EVERYONE LEAVES

EVERYONE LEAVES

Wendy Guerra

TRANSLATED BY ACHY OBEJAS

amazon crossing ⓒ

Everyone Leaves was awarded the first Bruguera

Novel Prize on March 2, 2006, by the sole juror,

acclaimed Catalan writer Eduardo Mendoza.

Text copyright © 2006 by Wendy Guerra
English translation copyright © 2012 by Achy Obejas

Everyone Leaves was first published in 2006 by Bruguera, Madrid, as *Todos se van*. Translated from Spanish by Achy Obejas. Published in English by AmazonCrossing in 2012.

"somewhere i have never travelled, gladly beyond" by e. e. cummings included here by kind permission of Liveright Publishing Corporation. *From E.E. Cummings: Complete Poems, 1904–1962*, edited by George J. Firmage. Liveright Publishing Corporation, copyright Trustees for the E.E. Cummings Trust, George James Firmage.

Published by AmazonCrossing
P.O. Box 400818
Las Vegas, NV 89140

ISBN-13: 9781612184333
ISBN-10: 1612184332
Library of Congress Control Number: 2012913255

We wouldn't have to give a moment's thought
to all this suffering if it weren't for the fact that
we're so worried about those we hold dear,
whom we can no longer help.

— **Anne Frank**, diary
November 19, 1942

I don't know exactly when I decided to stop being a child.

I've paid a high price, growing up all alone while everyone else left the island. They abandoned me, one after the other. These days, I can't be like just any other woman, because I don't belong to this world. The survival tools I was given are useless. I take refuge in my Diary; I only feel comfortable and normal within its pages. There, I'm always an adult pretending to be a little girl, although that isn't exactly true: I was always too adult for my Diary, too much a child for real life.

Ever since I learned to read and write, I have confessed into the Diary's pages. I hoped to grow, to take flight from the place I hid, trying to find freedom with a ticket out I still don't have. I'm not sure what's expected of me now. I started leaving pieces of myself behind as I was dragged from place to place. Now, sifted like sand everywhere, I'm not sure how to put my scattered world back together.

My parents aren't around anymore. They left, one at a time. That has more weight on my orphanhood than do the old rules by which they raised me. I'm intimidated by Cienfuegos, the city of my childhood: I'm haunted by the stories associated with my mother's file, the court case to get custody of me, and by my own file.

Reading the Diaries from my childhood and adolescence has been a painful journey. It has turned me inside out like a glove, except that once inside the glove, I discovered silk, which I'd never even noticed because I was so intent on tanning the hide on the outside so I could better sustain the blows of these last few years. The glove served as one more tool in the ring so I wouldn't fall. It was a random miracle I survived, protecting myself by posturing in ways alien to me.

To be born in Cuba is to learn to be absent from the world in which we live. I don't know how to use a credit card; the cashiers don't respond to me. A layover from one country to another can throw me off kilter, dislocate me, leave me breathless. When I'm outside, I feel in peril; indoors, I feel comfortably imprisoned.

I don't know when I let them take everything and leave me alone, naked, with the Diary in one hand and lipstick in the other, trying to paint my mouth a red that might be too much for this indefinite age.

The Childhood Diary

The homeland is childhood.

— **Charles Baudelaire**

Cura Lagoon, Cienfuegos, Cuba 1978

My mother has married a foreigner, a Swede who works at the Nuclear Center.

We live in a house on the lagoon, full of odd inventions like a rope that pulls on a set of strings and, using an anchor, lifts our shiny pots and pans out of the sea. The pots and pans are stored there so the salt will keep them clean. Fausto, my mother's husband, is very beautiful: blond and tall. He swims naked, walks around naked, reads the newspaper naked. It's always the same newspaper, the one in Swedish.

When the neighbors come to sell us black-market fish, it takes a lot for Fausto to get dressed. My mother threatens him by saying we'll go to jail. He puts on very frayed and rather scandalous jeans.

The neighbors love to talk about us. We live in an elegant neighborhood where the houses look out over the sea. But some, like ours, are loaned out by the state to foreigners like Fausto and overlook the lagoon. My mother doesn't want me to get too attached to this house, or to any house. Everything in life is on loan, that's the truth.

Material things don't matter, so I live as if I'm home visiting from boarding school. Anyway, I like it. Every afternoon I swim the distance from the lagoon to the sea. I throw my backpack down on the patio, take my school uniform off, and hang it on the hammock, then—*splash!*—into the water.

I'm a fish in a current that tries to drag me away, but I resist and take a long time to get back to the beach. I float lying still, letting the current take me where it wants. I'm part of a boat, a piece of glass, a broken doll, a freshwater fish flitting about, drifting aimlessly. And then salt gets in my mouth and reminds me to be careful, that I've washed into the bay.

Monday, November 13, 1978

My father came to visit after many months. He wasn't familiar with the house. He was aloof, suspicious, but he accepted a cup of coffee.

My mother showed him my notebooks, my grades, evidence that everything was fine. When he went to get me at the lagoon, he was outraged. When he saw us playing "killer whale" in the nude on the beach, he wanted to pummel Fausto. My father fumed; he couldn't take it. When we came up to greet him, he hit Fausto in the face hard—his hand even left a mark. I could see my father throwing punches in the water. Surprised by all this, Fausto couldn't figure out what was going on. My father screamed in his own defense, though no one was attacking him.

My father always ends up beating us. Never in public—he's always careful about that. But now he'd done it in front of the Swede. I was so embarrassed.

My father left and said he never wanted to see us again.

He left a cloud of rum all over the house. My mother doesn't know English or French well enough to explain things to Fausto the foreigner: "He hits us, that's all." Fausto falls asleep in bed with both of us. My mother looks like a little girl. She's crying. I feel older than my mother.

December 20, 1978

We don't see my mother much. She deals with sports and news off the wire for hours and hours on the radio. They say she's no longer trustworthy so she can't work on just news anymore. She broadcasts baseball games now.

They threaten to send her to Angola. I'm scared I'll be left alone with Fausto. I've never been without my mother. I don't understand why she can't meet the president of the German Democratic Republic just because Fausto is a foreigner. My mother says that's called racism. Racism isn't just about blacks, there are all kinds of racism.

I'm afraid my mother will go off to war.

I'd like to get terribly sick, perhaps with something incurable, so that they don't take her away. If I could just get sick. My mother says there's no reason for that war. But then she asks me to not repeat that to anyone.

I will die if they take my mother away. I will die of sadness.

She'll die from just about anything, she's so small—almost as small as me; she even has the same shoe size as me and borrows my stockings. She's not going to deal well with that war. My mother is more afraid of the outside than I am. She trembles when we're alone together, and she drops the flashlight whenever we hear a noise and goes looking for its source. She says it's not fear, just precaution, but I know very well it's a respectable kind of fear.

It makes me want to laugh. There are so many creatures beneath the waters. My mother's not going to be able to survive a real war.

I'm on a Diary strike because they sent my mother to war in Angola. This page is blank in her honor.

June 1979

My mother arrives tomorrow.

Fausto and I were alone for six months, waiting to hear her voice on the radio every afternoon reporting from Angola.

Fausto is Gulliver in a land of Lilliputians. I hug his beard, and he rocks me to sleep.

I don't care if anybody goes around in the nude.

I know the neighbors have complained and my father has made accusations. We have a court date soon; my mom doesn't know. When she gets home from the war tomorrow, we'll tell her. War and the trial, everything has come down around us all at once.

Fausto can't read Spanish all that well, so I had to explain what was on the document that arrived today. My father filed charges against my mother, accusing her of immorality, abandonment, and a few other things. He demands custody and full rights, that I be made his ward.

"Divide and conquer," Fausto tells me.

At dawn, when I see strange lights that I think are lightning, I get into bed with Fausto. He explains that it's a camera, that the flashes are made by someone watching us from afar.

"I'm a very dangerous Swede. You should be afraid of me— ooooh!" he says, making like a ghost as I dive under the quilt to hide from whoever is watching us. He tickles me silly. I fall asleep from laughter and fatigue.

Now I believe I'm being watched. I don't know if it's true or not, but it's crucial to be careful. I haven't done anything wrong in these last few months. I've behaved better than ever. I swear.

July 1979

My mother has come home from the war in Angola. Her skin is yellowish. She shakes and says they could come for her at any moment. She's much more scared than before.

She takes a lot of pills that Fausto brings her in bed. She doesn't have to go to work, so I read to her since she can't focus her eyes. She's very thin. My mother has come home sick from the war in Africa. She didn't want to go, and now she will never go back.

She says there will be no trial but Fausto winks at me, meaning that my mother is like a little girl who can't fathom what awaits us. I read her *The Book of Bolognese Marvels*, her favorite, by Eliseo Diego. I read it aloud, but I'm still when I see she's fallen asleep. Later, when she wakes, I patiently pick up where I left off.

My mother has to get well before I can go back to school. I don't want my friends to see her so weak. I don't like to see her like this. The veins on her legs and neck look like blue drawings. I know that parents can die when you're still a child, but I have to push that thought out of my mind.

War is a disaster. You should never be sent out to the fields to work or to war. It hurts me so much to see my mother breathing so badly. I can't stand to watch her sleep.

August 1979

My mom gets up every day and strolls around the patio. She's not yellowish anymore; she swims a little, sunbathes. She draws and hums old songs from Cienfuegos.

Ofelia had a little dish
that was the cutest, but it broke ooooh.
Pancho had to pay for what Rafael broke.

That's too much.

My friend Dania comes by every day to help us peel vegetables for lunch and put things in order.

Dania's my classmate. Her parents are doctors, and they're never home. She helps me pass my math tests. She lets her test paper fall to the floor and I do the same, then I erase her handwriting and write on top of it while she does the same and takes the test again. She solves all the problems and leaves the room before I do. I like helping her with composition because she doesn't like writing and I love making things up. She doesn't think I'm strange like the other girls do; she's very serious and doesn't laugh at my mother. She understands everything that's going on here, but she's very discreet.

The house feels like some sort of camp because Fausto leaves everything folded up in a row next to the wooden stairs. The house is like a little stone fortress. Fausto makes a path between the clean and dirty clothes. Dania and I climb on a bench to hang up the laundry that my mother washes ever so slowly.

Some friends from the puppet theater are coming over this afternoon. My mother wants to leave her radio job and go back to making puppets.

The pressure cooker has been on the stove since early today, and it's been hissing with all its might. The house smells like melted cheese.

Generoso and Magaly come in the back door. We extend that privilege exclusively to our friends. Magaly sees that my mother finally learned how to use the pressure cooker. We're all happy about that. Magaly helps her more or less straighten up the house. My mother finally reveals to everyone what she's been cooking: a plastic shoe. She wanted to melt it to create a base for a hand puppet.

My mother's friends are very still. And what if it had worked? Ah, well, then my mom would have gotten rich from melting shoes and making puppets. But so long as there's nothing to be gained from melting shoes, then my mom's just crazy. That's how people are in this town.

"A city of straight streets and twisted minds."

Fausto isn't coming home to sleep tonight; he has guard duty. Dania, Generoso, Magaly, my mother, and I all eat stone soup— the kind that has whatever our friends brought over and put into the broth. We're all together again, just like in the good old days. "Let the guests cook"—that's what my mom says. I love to find surprises in my soup.

Hot soup in August. Mosquitoes buzzing up from the lagoon. Fausto's lamp, the kerosene flame leaving a line of soot on the walls of the house. Our friends are with us like they used to be when we lived together, just the two of us. I feel better. We're finally getting closer to how it used to be.

My recipe for oyster cocktails:

Throw rocks at the patio walls.

Pull the shells out and open them with a knife.

Pull the oysters out of the shells.

Put them in a glass, then add tomato purée, lemon, and salt.

Drink them in one gulp.

September 1979

Gilberto Noda, the country singer, has died. He was witty and used profanities in his songs. He also played the guayo with Los Naranjos, the group that my mom helps out. Luís Gómez, the little old poet who always has a bottle in his back pocket, came to give us the news. They usually come here or go to our high-rise apartment to eat, drink, sing, and then leave. My mom records them at the station so she can play them during her programs. Very few people like that kind of thing anymore. They don't let them play live anymore because they have a tendency to say whatever's on their minds. Luís Gómez sings songs from Trinidad and tra-la-las. He used to sing me to sleep at the station with a song I learned by heart:

> *Death comes at night,*
> *tra-la-la*
> *to take its dress.*
> *Death comes slowly,*
> *tra-la-la.*
> *Flying through the scenery,*
> *on a gust of water and wine,*
> *tra-la-la.*

Death and its pain

take your fate,

tra-la-la.

It'll steal your lace,

if it doesn't take the right turn,

tra-la-la.

Death comes at night

and takes your fate,

tra-la-la.

That song scares me so much. It rings like a bell in my head. Whenever I hear it, it takes me a long time to go to sleep.

When we arrived at the wake, Gilberto was in a tub full of ice waiting for the box to arrive. I'd never seen a dead person, but he just looked asleep. I was curious so I looked at him about six times. He had on a dead man's tie and a dead man's suit. My mother put on her funeral dress—the black-and-white one—and I wore my marine blue dress, which is good for any occasion. My leather shoes and their Russian shoelaces don't really go together, but I made it work. When everyone started singing, Gilberto's wife and daughter cried more than ever. I didn't cry because he wasn't family.

Suddenly, the musicians called up Luís Gómez, but Luís was so drunk he could barely walk. The old guys started the song, slowly, so Luís could follow along…

Gilberto Noda died and now his widow cries.
Gilberto Noda died and now his widow cries.

Luís came to abruptly and joined in.

And what can we do? He's fucked now that he died.

Outraged, the family pulled out the machetes. And, nervous, my mother rushed me home. All dressed up. So here we are. She laughs and calls her girlfriends to tell them what happened. I'm very frightened and write while there's still light in the kerosene lamp, but there won't be enough for me to do my math homework.

At Dawn

It's late and dark. I'm writing by the light that comes in off the patio. Dead people don't frighten me that much. The only thing that really scares me is going to bars with my father. Getting up on one of those stools where my feet never touch the ground makes me dizzy; sometimes I even fall. There are drunks drinking in those greasy bars that smell of fried fish. We always have to flee because somebody throws a bottle and glasses start flying. They argue, but nobody knows what the other is trying to say. Sometimes they don't even talk before they start fighting. Bars are the worst places in the world. The smell that emanates from the drunks reminds me of dirty bathrooms. I never want to go back to the bars. I never want to go back, much less with my father.

The dead don't scare me. I realized that today at the wake. I'm much more frightened of drunks, of bars.

I can't sleep. I'm thinking of our court appearance and what awaits me if I get sent to live with my father.

October 1979

They still haven't set the date for the hearing, and Fausto got tired of wearing those stifling pants all the time. Now we pose for the neighbors.

When the lights go out, we paint our bodies with my watercolors, put on hats and masks, and light a bonfire at the edge of the lagoon. Our laughter can be heard on the other side, on the highway.

At seven in the morning, when I go to wake up my mother so that I won't be late for school, I see a drawing that she's made for me while she was half asleep. There's a poem under the drawing, too.

The girl sleeps, trapped between books
Who will come to free her tiny demons?
Who will come to defend her one day when
I put out my cigarette and wake her,
ending this dream once and for all?
A brief dream.
The girl sleeps, at the very least while I drew her.

October 1979

At dawn, Fausto spoke with my mother. I heard everything because I stayed up until they went to sleep. They fired him, and he can't live in Cuba anymore. We'll have to move to Sweden together.

Fausto says he hasn't broken any promises and that all he did was his job. He's going because of the Russians—because they don't take care of the nuclear plants in their country and they don't want him to report it. It seems that some of their plants are in bad shape and Fausto has a duty to let them know. I'm not sure I understand.

Fausto will go back to Stockholm, where there's more snow than anywhere else in the world, but I don't think my father will let me go. I know he'll say no. My father never wants what we want. My father is always getting between my mother and me. I always think my mother will go away because he's so obsessed with fighting with her. My mother is not very strong, this I know.

November 1979

My grades while my mother was in Angola were pretty bad. The school sent a report to the court saying that Fausto didn't take me to school on time in the morning and that I was absent a lot when my mother wasn't in Cuba.

They practically say they passed me out of pity. I'm what's called a "bad student." My head's in the clouds while everybody else is figuring out the square root of who knows what. I still don't know my multiplication tables.

My mom came back sick from Angola, with a nervous tic in her lips and a faraway look in her eyes. On her third day back, they set the court date, as if to make her crazy, but Fausto got a doctor's note so the lawyers could postpone it.

Now we can't change it again. We have to go to the hearing, which will be tomorrow. My mother ironed the blue dress, the one from the funeral.

Also, her black clothes, like always, and Fausto will wear his gray suit.

I'll stop seeing my mother tomorrow, I just know it. But I'll sleep with her tonight, all through the night.

November 1979

The Hearing

In court today, the room was full of strangers and friends of my father's. I heard them saying terrible things about my mother: "problematic," "difficult." Words such as "moral degradation in front of children." There were other things I don't remember now. Everything that was said about my mother was bad.

But there was praise for my father. The judge asked me who I wanted to live with. I stood up, alone, and looked straight at my father, who seemed to be about to explode. Suddenly I saw a little white feather in the corner of the window. It flew toward my face, and I blew it away with all my might. It touched Fausto's head and then my left hand. I blew at the feather like five times, but I didn't say anything. My father interjected and asked me if I wanted to live with him. I didn't want to say anything. My mother was there, but her eyes were an abyss. Like when she gets mad at me. Like when she doesn't want to hear from anybody.

Later, they showed pictures of Fausto and me. I looked good in some poses and bad in others. Fausto gazed at me happily while I searched for the little feather all over the courtroom, but I never found it again.

My mother and I left. She kissed my forehead and combed my hair again. She said one of her Protestant prayers and hugged me. She said I'd been very good, very well behaved. But I know I should have said I wanted to live with her. I'm so afraid of my father, I can't even talk. When I'm alone, I tell myself I'll do it, but I can never pull it off in his presence.

The verdict came down two hours later. For the next three years, I have to live with my father and his theater group up in the Escambray mountain range, far from the sea and the lagoon. Far from my mother and, of course, far from Fausto.

My mother and I have to say good-bye right then and there. There's no time. My father's coming for me. I ask my mother if I can see Fausto. She's crying. She can't understand what I'm saying. They finally bring Fausto over, and he opens his fist: he's rescued the white feather, which he'll keep to give to me as a gift when I go visit them.

The two of them came and said their farewells. My mother gave me my Diary and my school uniform in a bag. They'll send me my clothes later. I won't see her again for a month. Now everything's over. My father's waiting for me in the office.

A woman took me there by the hand, twice saying, "The revolution won't abandon you." I don't know what the revolution has to do with any of this. My father was waiting for me, sitting in the judge's chair. The woman gave him some papers to sign, and turned me over to him as if I were a package he'd gotten in the mail. My father hugged me tightly, and I thought I might scream if he didn't let go.

Through the window I saw Fausto outside, leading my mother very gently so she wouldn't fall apart. She was dazed.

They left. I saw them.

My father was very happy the rest of the day. His friends celebrated with him. He won and we lost.

December 1979

The theater group in the mountains is very small. They live between two hills, like a valley, full of sunflowers and coffee plants. There are just a few houses and an L-shaped dormitory where the unmarried people stay. They've moved us to the third house. We're a family of two.

Some friends have come to give me gifts: barrettes and ribbons for my hair, which won't hold anything because it's as straight as Chinese hair. There's a woman who wants to win me over; she's probably seeing my father. But she's afraid of him, like me. She greets me in a low voice and runs off.

My father thinks he can avoid talking to me about the problem—the hearing—and about the days I can go be with my mother. Everything has been silent. I wanted to write when we were in the car, but he took the notebook from me and told me we had to sleep. He doesn't like my Diary so I've had to hide it. My father calls me by my surname. The smell of the food here is strange. I'm not hungry; I don't want to eat.

The house is well-lit because there are many more windows than walls. There's a room for us and one that remains shut. I've already been warned about it. The kitchen is very small—it looks like it belongs in a dollhouse. Ants march on the counter all the way up to the ceiling. In the living room, there's a shelf full of crafts from all over the world, but there's not a single book in this entire house. This strikes me as very odd. There are no paintings and no photos, either.

This house looks like a place where no one lives for very long. Perhaps we'll move soon.

Tonight I'll see one of the plays the group puts on for the peasants.

December 1979

I can only write when my father's not around. He's already told me that a Diary isn't very discreet.

My mother should be coming for my birthday, but they won't let Fausto get anywhere near me. As if the Swede were an ogre, when in fact he's sweet as a puppy.

My father has forbidden me from seeing Fausto. That's what he said when I asked at breakfast.

I start school this afternoon. I already have a new uniform.

There's another girl roughly my age with the theater group. She's always hanging around the chickens. She's the magician's daughter. He's deaf. My throat hurts, and I'm afraid of going to school with her. She's two years older, so she'll be ahead of me. When the milk truck comes, my father will get on with me and take me to the rural school. I don't have my books here; they've probably turned everything in to the authorities in Cienfuegos. I didn't have time to get my notebooks.

I'm lonely. My mother doesn't call. Is it that they don't let her talk to me on the phone? They must be doing something terrible to her over there. When you're little, you're taken advantage of because you don't have money to go see your friends or hire a lawyer to defend your mother. When I'm bigger, I'll never keep quiet. I swear I'm not going to be as weak as she is. I'm going to take care of her. I'm going to defend her against my father and his lawyers.

December 1979

I don't know if I should write this in the Diary. I'm scared. I can't tell anybody about it. Please keep my secret.

My father slept with a woman in our bed. He came out of the room and punished me by making me stand behind the bathroom door. I saw everything they did. I couldn't move because he kept looking at me, and I knew he was punishing me. My father wasn't naked. He pulled his pants down and rubbed against her. She didn't have clothes on and screamed very loudly.

I wanted to leave, but my father got up and I stood still and straight as a flagpole. Time passed. They sweated, chatted, and breathed heavily. I was scared to look at what they were doing. A few times, I closed my eyes. When it was finally over, my father stood up and dragged me to the shower. He closed the curtain. As the water ran, he told me never to trust any man. I'd never seen my father naked. He touched my hair, and I ran out soaking wet. That's when the woman realized I'd been in the bathroom the whole time and started screaming. I ran to the highway and thought about everything all day long. It's night now. I know I can't trust anyone.

"Margaret Thatcher is the head of the British government and a woman to be feared." That's what I hear my father say when I walk by and he's arguing politics and drinking with his friends. Apparently there are also women who can't be trusted.

I'm going to bed. My father doesn't trust anyone or anything. The bed smells of perfume and sweat. I take the sheet off and sleep on the mattress. I hope tonight I won't dream.

December 1979

The kids at school are way ahead of me. They're on their third science lesson, and I'm on the second. Everyone looks at me a little horrified. A black boy asked me if I was a foreigner and I told him I was from Cienfuegos. When the teacher introduced me, they all laughed; it must be because I wear sandals with no socks. I didn't bring my school shoes. I didn't have time to go get them from my house.

When I got out of school the first day, my father was already at the door. He hadn't gone back to the theater group, he'd stayed in Manicaragua drinking rum with some of the old guys. He told me this, but I also saw the old guys. I got scared because he's a different person when he drinks. But today he just helped me up on the workers' truck, which they call a guarandinga, and everything was fine. The truck ride was bumpy all the way home. There's no power now, but I told him I have to do my homework. The food isn't ready. Luckily, I'm not hungry and I'm in no hurry to do my homework during this blackout. My father says he'll go to the theater group's dining hall and get food for me.

I'm falling asleep. What could Fausto and my mother be doing right now? There's probably no power there either.

December 1979

My father didn't come home yesterday. I woke up hungry at about four in the morning. His watch was in the bathroom. I drank some orange juice I found in the refrigerator and laid down in our bed. I have to sleep with him.

My legs are covered with mosquito bites. I can't stand the itching.

It's early now, and I'm going to go eat in the dining hall with the actors because there's nothing for breakfast in the house. I hope my father doesn't get mad, but I'm very hungry. I put on yesterday's uniform.

The Escambray is very pretty. There's a cloud of yellow butterflies hovering above the table on the patio. The sunflowers are still asleep, and everybody's walking on the path outside the bedroom window. The entertainment starts at nine. I have to hurry.

December 1979

My father got home at six in the evening. He sat down at the table and drank and wrote without once looking me in the face. He forbade my going to the dining hall, but he didn't yell at me. He just talked to me very seriously.

I've been out on the patio all day. I went by a few of the actors' homes but they're all rehearsing their plays. If it's true I can't go to the dining hall unless I'm with my father, they'll tell on me and they won't let me in. I came back in the house because it's raining a lot. I know where the telephone is now, and I wish I could run away and call my mother.

I didn't go to school today because I can't get on the truck by myself. The other girl, Elena, waved good-bye, and I smiled when I saw her leave with her mother. I thought about asking them to take me with them, but I wasn't sure what my father would say.

Until very recently we slept together, but the smell of moonshine was killing me. Everything smells bad in that room.

I was thinking of writing to my mother, but I don't know where the post office is, and I don't have money for stamps.

The school is very poor and very small. Compared to the huge house in Cienfuegos, it's like a shack. My mother would love to see this little school.

My father snores. He hasn't given me anything to eat. I'll go get food from the theater group. I'm really hungry. My stomach hurts, but he'll get mad if I wake him.

December 1979

My father always forgets to take me to eat, and I can only leave this wooden house when there's a group activity or when he takes me to school. And he doesn't always take me: in the last two weeks, he's only taken me six times.

He doesn't let me talk too much with the other members of the theater group. He says my mother let me develop the bad habit of talking to adults. But he doesn't let me go play with Elena either, and he doesn't let Elena come to our house. She and I send each other messages with a pair of slingshots her brother made. Her brother is fifteen and goes to boarding school out in the country. I saw him Saturday morning in the dining hall. He has a blue uniform and tie. Elena prints when she writes, but I'm still using script. My printing looks uneven. I don't like it, I like cursive better. I love sending Elena messages.

When I finally talked to my mother in secret, she said that was something prisoners do. She always exaggerates. I thought my mother was crying when we talked. She was afraid my father would catch us talking so we hung up really fast.

It was six in the morning, and I couldn't sleep. I used the telephone in the hallway with the lock on it. Someone had unlocked it. It looked like they were probably going to make a call at dawn.

Fausto blew me a lot of kisses because we don't really understand each other on the phone, so it was just kisses and more kisses. My mother choked so as not to cry; I know this about her. She said she's coming for my birthday. She asked me many times if my father had hit me. I told her no, but she doesn't believe me. As far as my mother is concerned, things are always worse than they seem. I hung up and came back to our room. My father wasn't back yet. When he got home, he'd brought me candy and some yogurt. I pretended to be asleep.

December 1979

At school today, I was asked why I don't go every day like the other kids (the teacher said, "Like the other Pioneers"). I told her my father forgets to bring me sometimes. I'm waiting for him to come. They're surely going to scold him, and then he'll scold me. I'm gonna get it! But I didn't know what else to say. That's the way it is. My father forgets that he has to bring me to school at quarter to one on the milk truck. There's no way I'm ever on time for my afternoon classes.

I'm waiting for the guarandinga to show up with my father. It's incredible—it's almost six o'clock and Elena already left with her mother. My teacher and the principal are also waiting for my father. It's raining really hard. The school lights are on. The rain leaks on the desk, where there's a bucket that rattles when the drops fall into it. My teacher checks my notebook to see how many days I've come to school and how many I've been absent.

My father finally showed up, his hair loose, shirt open, and trousers torn. The teacher said I should go directly to the classroom and write "I'm a revolutionary Pioneer who goes to school every day" one hundred times.

I've never not wanted to come. I don't understand why I'm being punished; they should make my father write this. There's no way anyone can write that sentence a hundred times on the black-board anyway. It's too small.

When we got home, my father told me he had to set the rules. First, I couldn't respond if anyone asked anything about him. Second, I had to say I was sick whenever I didn't go to school. And, third, I couldn't tell anybody whether I'd eaten or not. I would be punished now for talking to my teacher, so no dinner again for me. My father took a bottle out of the wardrobe, refilled the one in his pants, and locked me in the house. He said everything in a very low and angry voice.

He left. There's no power today, either. I don't know how I'll be able to stand the darkness. I feel like crying, but I don't want to cry.

I know my father would explode.

December 1979

My father didn't come home to sleep for two days. I ran away to the dining hall. I was about to faint—I'd only been drinking sugar water. I couldn't take it anymore. He's here now, so I have to put this away.

...They reprimanded him because I went to the dining hall alone and asked for food, telling the supervisor I hadn't eaten in two days. They gave me several things, but my stomach's upset and all I can eat is the egg and rice. I brought the milk home with me for when I go to bed.

I was just sitting here staring straight ahead as if it was an old habit. It had been three days since I'd been to school. Then my father hit me, out of the blue, and my head smashed against the table. I thought I'd lost an eye. He came up from behind me without saying a word. I knew he'd beat me, I just knew it. But there's nothing I can do.

He hit me on the head, hard, with his belt buckle—really hard. He grabbed and pulled my hair and got two fistfuls, which are now in my notebook. He smashed my ear against the table. The buckle hurt and the wooden table sounded like it was going to crack. I bled a lot because the metal in the buckle pierced my scalp. It was hard to get out. It seemed like the hole was huge, but in fact it was small.

I was totally dazed. I don't even remember what he was yelling about. I don't even remember why he said he hit me. Surely it was because I said I hadn't eaten.

When he slammed the door and my dizziness passed, I found the rum in the wardrobe and poured it on my head. That's what my mother does whenever she gets a cut. I only used a little, so he won't notice.

Then I got under the faucet. My right cheek is swollen, and I can't hear so well out of my left ear. My mouth is puffed up, too. I'm afraid of going to the dining hall. But I'm hungry; my belly sounds like the horns they play at the concerts in the park.

I went to Elena's house and knocked on the bedroom window for her mom. She used some Mercurochrome on my cut. She didn't even ask me what had happened. I think she knows. I told her I was very hungry, and she gave me a guava shake and bread with croquettes. I sat in the doorway to eat. That's when I started crying.

Elena's mom's name is Chela. She got nervous and told Elena to bring me a cold glass of water, with ice. She asked how she could help me. I told her to please not tell anyone I'd been there. She started to cry.

She told me she wanted to give me a haircut and I said yes. My black hair fell bit by bit to the floor. My hair is just like my mother's. It's best that she cut it because otherwise my father will keep pulling it. It hurts less if he can't grab it. Chela cut my hair really short. Elena brought me over to the mirror. I look like a little boy, but I don't care. At least I'm all fresh and clean.

Later, I went home. I went inside to study, which really means staring at the doodles I copied from the faded olive-green chalkboard. When my father takes me to school—the few times I've been—I just copy everything down without understanding any of it. School used to be a nightmare before, but now I really like going—at the very least to see the other kids.

I'd like to spend hours and hours with the teacher. But I don't understand a thing, and to top it off, I can't hear very well out of my left ear.

December 1979

My father didn't like seeing me with short hair at all. He hit me again, and again on my face, but not so hard this time. He slapped me a few times because he doesn't want me to go to Elena's house. He doesn't understand how I got a haircut without his permission, and he's forbidden me telling anyone that he's hit me even one time. He says Elena's mom is a gossip and a lost soul. He says I look like a boy with my hair short.

I left the house as soon as he fell asleep. I threw myself down to rest with the chickens. I made a little house for myself between the trees. I dragged an old mattress I'd found in the gym to my Little Forest. That's what I call my hideout: the Little Forest.

I know my mother is coming tomorrow, because tomorrow I turn nine years old.

I found a little mirror shard in the patio. I look very pale. I don't want to look like a boy but, as my mother says, circumstances dictate.

December 1979

It's been three weeks since I've seen my mother. Today is my birthday and she's come all the way here to see me.

As soon as I saw her, I burst into tears even though I'd told myself I wouldn't cry when she got here. Luckily, my father wasn't around. I didn't dare ask about Fausto. But I write Fs all over my notebooks. In the bathroom, when I'm going number two, I write F F F invisibly all over the gray cement floor. I'm afraid I'm being spied on.

My mother saw my bruises and began to cry. She wanted to talk to the group's director to get me out of here, but I didn't let her. I can take it. I'm going to be good so he doesn't have to beat me. My mother says I haven't done anything wrong, but I think I must have because everybody always does something wrong. That's why he hit me. That's the way he is, and I just have to put up with it until he decides to let me go home. Surely he'll get bored soon, that's what I told my mother. He can't deal with so much responsibility. My mother cracked up when I said that. She kissed me heartily and took things out of a bag she'd brought.

My mother is not doing well. She's skinnier than usual, and her Swedish clothes are worn. I saw her when she reached the top of the hill. She brought some of those weird foods that F cooks using curry and olive oil, nutmeg, and steak sauce. He uses all that in his food. My mother says F, in case someone's listening in on us. My father can't bear to even hear his name.

My mom visited with me for three hours, until my father showed up and screamed at her that she was crazy and that we have food here. My mom got scared and said good-bye right away. She left me some of her books. "Don't study if you don't want to," she told me, "but read these so that I can bring you other books the next time I come."

My father said there was no visit scheduled next week.

My mother kissed my forehead and went up the hill, whimpering, walking briskly, being sure to greet the people from the theater.

My father sniffed the food and threw it down the toilet. He flushed and laughed at me.

December 1979

He didn't leave me anything to eat again today.

Chela brought me a cake in the morning because, as she was leaving, my mother told her I had turned nine. My father tossed it onto the patio. The chickens ate it. From the window, I saw them pecking at it. There are seven hens and twelve chicks.

Now I won't ever eat again. That's it.

December 1979

I haven't eaten again. I don't need to try—I'm not even hungry anymore. When my father forces me, I just vomit everything back up. I vomit it because I want to, not because my stomach's upset.

And, in any case, I'm disgusted by the smell of moonshine on him every night. I can't even drink my milk because of it, and that's the only thing I'll even taste. He twists my ear until I swallow, but after I swallow I go to the bathroom and vomit until a little bit of blood comes up. That means there's nothing left. When I flush, the water swirls like the whirlpool back in the lagoon. I used to spend a lot of time there. If you hold on and swim, you get tossed out in the ocean, where everything is calmer and there's no whirlpool. When I throw up, I feel better. My stomach doesn't do flips anymore, and I know I'm winning this battle with my father, who refuses to let me eat the food F sends me.

December 1979

Today my father took me to the puppet theater, where they were performing one of his plays. It's about a little goat who can't find her way home and gets lost in the prairie.

The puppets are huge, grotesque, and the actors wear enormous costumes with custom-made heads. They also have giant shoes attached to their feet with some sort of rubber bands. They leap about, sing, dance, and invite the children on the stage to take part in the play. It's very pretty, with many lights and smoke that comes from behind the plants.

I like what my father does, but I don't like him.

On the way home, he asked me if I wanted to be in a play. I said yes. I'll do anything to get out of that wooden house. My father hasn't had a drink today, which is why he's so nice, but my mother would tell me not to trust him anyway. I won't go to sleep until he drifts off first.

December 1979

My father's friend—the one who's afraid of him—came to see me. She brought me a letter from my mother. She watches out the window to see if anyone's coming while I read it.

> *My sweet girl:*
>
> *I came home very distressed after our visit because you're so thin and anxious. I beg you not to keep anything from me. If anything happens to you and I know about it, it'll be a lot easier to get you help and to be together again. Please let Maricela know what's going on with you; we've been friends since our days together at the National School of Art. Let's do this: Whenever you're near the telephone and it's unlocked, call me, let it ring twice and then hang up. I'll call you right back. Just be patient by the phone and that way we'll be able to talk once in a while. My love, try to eat what they serve you and try to enjoy it as much as you can in the moment. I know your father forgets sometimes, but I don't think he's doing it intentionally. That's just the way he is. Look at how skinny your mom is these days. Keep eating so you can read and write whatever you like.*
>
> *Neither one of us is in a great place right now. Remember the story I always tell you: Once upon a time, there was a prince who had been turned into a hobo. He'd fallen asleep in a doorway in old England,*

where he was shivering in the horrible cold. Then he felt a wave of heat. Suddenly, a mouse jumped from the lining of his coat. The prince was shocked that he'd been sleeping with a creature that he so despised. He went to see the sunrise. He looked up at the sky, which was still filled with stars, and said, "Look at what's happened to me, at how low I've sunk, that I've become a prince who sleeps with mice. Things have to change." And so they did.

This too shall pass. Keep up your reading; read anything and everything, and do your best at school. Don't do anything that will upset your father, and send me a letter now and then via Maricela. I can't go see you until next Sunday according to the agreement with the lawyers.

Take care of yourself and be a strong little girl. Remember that you can disinfect your wounds with alcohol. Maricela can always give you some if you need it, as well as any medicines—just ask her. F sends you much love and many tickles. For the moment, everything's fine here at the lagoon. We miss you very much, very, very much, my sweetie. Please tear this letter up as soon as you read it, don't let anyone see it.

A big kiss from your mom, who loves you more than ever.

P.S. Nieve, don't talk to your father about us. Keep it to an absolute minimum. Remember that everything irritates him. A big kiss, my dear. Take very good care of yourself.

December 1979

I'm in greater danger inside this house than outside. As soon as I get home, I get a queasy feeling in my stomach, and I start to shake. I'd rather stay in the Little Forest, even if it gets dark. My mother says the door to our home is sacred, but this is not my home. Sometimes I try to count all the houses I've lived in since I was born, but I don't have enough fingers on my hands and I have to use my toes too.

My head itches. I think the chickens in the Little Forest where I sleep on my little bed have given me green fleas. I'm going to ask Chela to check my head because I can't see anything in the mirror.

Today I came home from school with Elena and the magician. My father lets me do that now because otherwise I'd just rot waiting for him to pick me up.

There's a room in the wooden house that I've never been able to go into because it's locked shut. But today the keys are in the lock and I'm just waiting for my father to go off to the Hotel Hanabanilla so I can sneak in and see what's in there.

I used my slingshot to send Elena a message to see if Chela was going to come over and check my head because I'm itching everywhere now.

My mother brought me various books: one by Enid Blyton (the Englishwoman); another book by Jules Verne (who ran away from home when he was eleven and became a cabin boy and sailor before he got caught by his parents); *Roman Elé* by Nersys Felipe (I like this one a lot; it makes me want to go swimming in the Cuyaguateje, which is Crucita and Roman Elé's river and which is very far from the Escambray); *Memoirs of a Cuban Girl Who Was Born with the Century* by Renée Méndez Capote; *The Book of Bolognese Marvels* by Eliseo Diego, my mom's favorite. She's lent it to me for a few days.

My mother wrote something in the Eliseo Diego book, under the dedication: "For my little daughter, who is far away, though we continue to be two peas in a pod." My mother can be very funny. Eliseo's dedication to her is long and written in a very small and fine script. (It's private, so I won't copy it here.)

I have a lot to read so I shouldn't pay attention to whatever's going on outside.

December 1979

I'm riddled with green fleas. I knew it. Chela poured the whole
bottle of kerosene on my head. They tried to pluck the fleas out one
by one, but those nits can't be yanked out just like that. They're
probably going to kick me out of school. I've been absent too much
and I won't pass this year.

I asked Elena to stay with me; whenever I ask her a favor, I call
her Elenita. She likes it and she stays. We made some snow cones
with mandarin oranges from the patio because there's a fridge in
my house and hers is broken. Chela keeps a lookout for my father
so we won't get caught. He doesn't like it at all that they visit. My
mother says my father is antisocial.

Elena and I finally broke into the closed room. It's small and
has only one window. We were stunned because it's full of pictures
of my mother from when she was young. I'd never seen the wedding photos: she's wearing a white miniskirt and a veil. My father
wears a very well-pressed gray suit. He's placed dried flowers by the
pictures of my mother. The worst part is a rag doll with my mother's
name embroidered on her chest that's stuck full of needles. They're
so bunched up, there's no room for even one more needle. Elenita
says that's really intense brujería. There are also coconuts and what
looks like a head, with eyes and a mouth, over in the corner by

the window. There are fruits around it and melted candles, and chocolate candies, too. But Elena says we can't touch them, that if our hands go near them, we'll be cursed, that bad luck will follow us for the rest of our lives.

My father puts spells on my mother. There's not a single photo of me in the entire room. I'm in a state of shock and can't seem to move out of here. I'm writing this on the floor. This room feels out of this world. There are like ten puppets hanging from the ceiling. I think my mom made them for a production of *Peter Pan* when I was born.

Chela called Elena for dinner so I'm alone now. I just stared at the photos and got a bellyache. I don't know if that stuff will actually hurt my mother. Still, it can't be a good thing that somebody thinks that much about you, even when you're far away. I wish I could run away like Jules Verne and go very, very far. The room smells of funeral flowers.

I grabbed the doll and pulled the needles out one by one and threw them out the window. From now on, the doll sleeps with me.

December 1979

I fell asleep on the floor and by the time I registered the door crashing open, my father had already found me in the forbidden room. He was furious. He came at me with a leather belt. He'd oiled it about a week ago, so it was reddish and cracked and slithered and stung where it hit me.

I was so sleepy I couldn't quite tell what was going on. But when he realized it didn't hurt all that much, he pulled on my ear until he made my little Mallorca pearl earring fall out, the one F bought me on his Christmas vacation. My father split my ear in two; I bled like never before. My ear still hurts, and since it was the same ear as before, I didn't hear what he said very well. But he made me swallow the pearl. He forced it into my mouth and didn't let me go until he saw that I'd swallowed.

After he dished out what he thought I deserved, he went to bed and fell asleep without a care.

My mother had told me not to contradict him, not to go against him, so this is my fault.

I went to ask Maricela for the alcohol but she was out on a pass. Today is Saturday, there's no one here. If I ask Chela, she'll freak out.

Dear Diary: Tomorrow will be another day.

December 1979

They let me go to school even though I have fleas. I have to wear a very tight kerchief around my head, which means I hear the teacher even less, but I'd rather go anyway instead of staying here. I can make out the teacher's words by how she moves her lips, though when I look at the numbers, they're Greek to me.

I let my thoughts wander far, far away, as far as I can get from here. Sometimes I ask myself why the whirlpool in the lagoon never slows down; I wonder what makes the water swirl like that. No matter when you go swimming, it's moving around. Maybe it's true that inside it is a magical imp, like the one Feijóo told us about when he came to visit. Maybe he lives in the whirlpool and nobody can see him because he goes out at night and there are no lights around the lagoon. One day that black imp will grab me by the foot and drag me down for being so curious. I always try to stay in the whirlpool, to not get tossed into the ocean, so I can splash around in the circling waters.

They made me take a math test but I left it blank. I got 100 on a Spanish test a week ago. The principal told me I could get help with the math test if I wrote something for the ceremonies January 1.

These are the phrases I have to use. It's like writing an essay, just like the one on the test, but full of patriotic things:

Pioneers José Martí.

Pioneers Moncada Barracks.

XXI Anniversary of the Triumph of the First Socialist Revolution in the Americas.

Guerrilla warfare.

The future.

One hundred percent promotion.

The triumph of the nation's glorious January.

Despotic and brutal imperialism.

The sugar harvest and coffee production.

Times of peace.

The miracle of the revolution.

Homeland or death, we shall triumph.

Elenita and I called Cienfuegos from the front office. That phone's on a hook and you have to ask for the operator. We were able to get through from our hideout. It took a lot of doing, and I had to whisper the whole time, but I told my mother everything.

I had to wait out her crying and then I changed the subject and she calmed down. I asked her what "despotic and brutal" meant. I told her I got picked to write an essay to be read during the January 1 celebrations. My mother said that the homeland is one thing and politics are another, and to be careful what I write. She also said I have to look closely when I go number two to see if I can find F's pearl, that I can't lose it. My ear is flapping loose; there's no hole to hold an earring anymore. It'll be best to just give it to her when she comes so she can keep it.

She also said that the next time my father beats me, I should tell the group leader and complain. That way maybe the lawyers will let me go back home with her.

F started to tell me a bunch of weird stuff in Spanish and Swedish. Then I had to hang up because a teacher was coming.

December 1979

It's December 24. My mother came to see me and brought me a pastry that F baked for me. It's delicious. My father left as soon as she arrived. They didn't even greet each other. I told my mother, very slowly, about the room with the brujería. She laughed it off and didn't give it much importance. Then she said something that seems to make a lot of sense: "If a doll stuck full of needles is more powerful than my own mind, then I should just go ahead and put a bullet in my brain. Those things aren't our problem, Nieve." She doesn't believe in any of that. She believes in the power of her own mind, and so do I. She says the worst thing about my father is his obsessions.

My mother doesn't want me to write the essay for the ceremony on January 1, but I have to. She doesn't know that's how I'm going to pass math. Besides, who's going to find out? That little school is so far from everything.

My mom tried to help me with the essay but she got angry every time we had to use one of the required phrases. She can't deal with it.

I finally told her more or less what happened to my ear, but I didn't give her details because otherwise she'll cry.

We came to an agreement. The next time he so much as touches me, I'll run out and tell everybody what's going on. This can't go on. I ate everything she brought me, although my throat's a little raw from all the vomiting. My mom sang me a Christmas song and gave me a teddy bear that F sent as a present. I have to hide it so my father won't guess who it's from.

By the time she left, she was a lot calmer. She didn't cry. She asked me to remember our agreement.

She did scold me, though, because I hadn't finished reading any of the books she brought me last time. That made her sad.

We hugged for a while and sang a song we both like: "The Umbrella Dance." She sings the boy's part and I sing the girl's.

ME:
Because he's a domestic saint
who receives petitions for marriage
Saint Anthony is overwhelmed
and I don't want to
ask for that much,
just one true love.

MY MOM:
Miss, I'm single and in love,

I think you're pretty,

so pretty I'm stunned,

I can't believe

you don't have a man at your side.

ME:

Oh, you're such a talker!

MY MOM:

I am a Spanish gentleman.

ME:

I'm no stranger.

MY MOM:

Open your umbrella

so the sun won't die of jealousy.

Everything's different with my mom. Things are a little crazy—
it's true what my father says and I wouldn't deny that. But I love her
craziness. Life with her isn't normal, but it's not normal with him
either, and I don't like normal lives anyway.

In the shadow of a lacy silk umbrella
love sings softly
In the shadow of an umbrella
there are dreams, madrigals, a soft voice
la la la la, la la la, laaaaaaaaaaaaaaaaaaaaaa

December 1979

I'm still having problems with my father and food. He never brings me anything to eat, and when he finally does, he forces me to eat even if it's three or four in the morning.

I'm going to exaggerate everything that happens, even if that makes me the biggest liar in the world.

He hits me, but not hard enough to bruise me. If he goes a while without hitting me, I'm going to throw myself against the bars in the gym and then say he hit me.

Maybe I'll be able to go home in January. I'm not going to do anything, but if he hits me again, I have a plan to get out of here.

December 1979

It's December 31. My father went to get a small pig to roast for those of us who've stayed behind without a pass. Even Elena got to go to Havana with her parents. I'm dying to go to Havana. Elena's going to bring me photos when she comes back, so I'll see the Malecón. They say that my grandparents live just beyond the Malecón, about ninety miles from there. No one can swim that far. You can only come and go on a boat or in a plane.

I finally finished the essay, and I'm going to copy it to my Diary so I won't forget it. It's not hard for me to write in my Diary, but writing on command takes me hours and hours.

Comrades:

We, the Pioneers José Martí, wearing red headscarves, join the Pioneers Moncada, wearing blue headscarves, in celebrating the XXI Anniversary of the triumph of the first Socialist Revolution in America. Although we don't understand what's being said about guerrilla warfare, we are ready to do battle side by side with our parents, our brothers and sisters, and all the family who love us and work so hard for our future.

We will achieve 100 percent promotion while we study in our schools during times of peace.

A glorious January triumph is our hope.

Imperialism, so despotic and brutal, will not reach our schools because we, the children, are grateful and always on guard.

We the Pioneers are sure that the sugar harvest and coffee crop will be very good this year because it is raining to fulfill the miracle of the revolution.

And now, a poem:
The rain is so important
to our economy.
It eliminates droughts,
makes our seas swell,
and the palms that adorn
this land of ours bloom.
And what made our land
a little less beautiful before,
now turns into a stunning vista
with butterflies and flowers;
the cities and the fields
turn colorful.
Homeland or death, we shall triumph.
—5th Grade Pioneers, Battle of Escambray School,
Manicaragua, Villa Clara

I really hope I pass math after this. I wasn't asked for the poem but I like finishing off with it.

If my mother ever reads this…

Tuesday, January 1, 1980

It's January 1.

They came to get us with a tractor. Now we're jostling all the way to school. I'm dizzy because the tractor moves from side to side, as if it were going to go over the guardrails. My father didn't come home last night. I didn't eat dinner or breakfast. New Year's Eve was just another night. The ceremonies had started when I arrived, my uniform all wrinkled.

The principal tied my headscarf on real tight. She parted my hair with a comb that stank; before that, she wet my hair to get it into some kind of shape because it's usually pretty rebellious right after I wake up. Then she stood me up on a rock in the patio so I could read aloud.

I read the essay but I don't think it went over well. There was a lot of discussion among the people who came from Villa Clara. They're making me wait, grounded in the office until my father comes to get me.

It seems that what I wrote wasn't right, but I wrote what I was asked. Maybe the problem was the poem; that must be it. I shouldn't have included the poem. I always do more than I should. If my mother had been here, I wouldn't have gotten it wrong.

I don't know when my father will get here. It's late. I'm weak.

I'm taking a math test this afternoon but I can't figure it out. The numbers all look like little animals to me—insects, worms. I don't understand anything.

I'm still waiting for my father. I'd like a little bit of sugar water.

I have to put my Diary away. There shouldn't be any open notebooks while I'm taking this test. It's getting dark.

In the Wooden House

Now it's a real disaster. The teacher is at the wooden house with me. She fell asleep in the living room, sitting in a rocking chair. My father is still not here and it's very late. He's been missing two days now. The teacher herself went to get food for me from the group. I asked her to please leave because my father is going to kill me if he sees her here with me. She smiled and stroked my head.

She laughs because she doesn't understand, she can't imagine how things are, or how he gets when he drinks.

Then, little by little, she helped me with the answers on the math test. She read me the questions one part at a time so she could explain what I had to write down, why and how we arrived at those numbers. It feels like magic when I understand things and can respond on my own.

She asked me a lot of questions. I answered as little as possible; my mother had warned me before the hearing that I couldn't talk at all once I got here. She says that in our country if you say the least little thing it gets blown up very easily and taken the wrong way.

I'm going to go sleep in the hammock in the dining room. I feel sorry for my teacher.

Friday, January 4, 1980

Dear Diary:

I'm sorry for not writing for two days. I can't open one of my eyes, and my right arm hurts. I can write with either hand but I just didn't feel like focusing my eyes. My father came home drunk and tore the place apart. He beat me up right in front of the teacher. The teacher called everyone to see, screamed, and left the house threatening him. As soon as she told him I had ideological problems, my father exploded, he wanted to kill us both. He kept talking and talking about my mother, he said the most horrible things about my mother even though she's so far away.

Everything happened because of the essay I wrote. I've read it a thousand times, but I don't get what the problem is.

They just had a meeting demanding that my father let me go home or send me to boarding school. I hope I get to go home. They said next time they won't put up with his hitting me.

I know what I'm going to do. I'm going to leave this place and not wait to get beat up again. I'm a real sight. Chela's taking care of my eye; she cries while she deals with it.

I don't even want to call my mom.

Saturday, January 5, 1980

I don't care that my father's calm now. I went to the gym and I hit myself over and over against the bars. I threw myself from the little water tower and scraped my knees. I bled from one of the bruises on my forehead like never before. For the first time, I went to see the director, who's a very tall, very famous man. When he saw me bleeding, he was horrified. He immediately got his car ready to take me home to my mother. He said he's deciding what's right because otherwise my father's going to kill me.

"I don't know what's worse, a lunatic mother or an alcoholic father," he said very loudly to everyone who was a witness to his decision. I have to look up *lunatic* to see what it means.

I am now the biggest liar in the world but I don't care. Nobody knows what's a lie and what's real.

I'm on my way to Cienfuegos with the director in his car. Chela's with us too. I'm writing in my Diary. My mother will be terrified when she sees us, but she'll be happy when she finds out I'm staying with her and Fausto forever.

Good-bye to the yellow butterflies, to the sunflowers, to the ants, to the dolls, to the little school, and the milk truck. I didn't want to say good-bye to Elenita because she's very sentimental and cries over any little thing.

I left my school uniform at the wooden house. I forgot everything. It must be because of the beatings. My head is hazy, or maybe it was just because I was in a hurry to get out of there before the ogre came home.

I traded all the truths for one lie, and because of that one lie, I get to go home, finally.

...As we were crossing Manicaragua, we saw my father. He had his arm around Maricela, my mother's friend. I almost died. The director stopped the car and got out. My father tried to slap him. He was drunk. I thought my heart would pop out of my chest.

When we were finally leaving, my father stuck his head in the car and said I wouldn't be able to stay with my mother, that he'd notify the appropriate authorities.

I think I fainted from fright. Now we're entering Cienfuegos. The whole city is reflected in the bay, upside down.

Friday, January 11, 1980

It's a long story.

It's already January 11. I haven't been able to write because I didn't have my notebook. I'm writing on the backs of the ones they gave me, which are square. I'll glue the pages to my Diary later, whenever I get it back. Everything has happened so fast.

They didn't let me stay home. My mother didn't want me to either, which is why I'm at this Center for the Reeducation of Minors.

It's five thirty in the morning and I get up before the other kids so I can write. Everything's pretty strict here. It's dark, and I'm taking advantage of the little bit of light that comes from the teachers' bathroom so I can write in my bed, which is in the right corner of the room.

When I got home, my mom was playing on the patio with Dania, my little friend. My mother would toss the pick-up-sticks, and the two of them would gather them up together. That's how she played with me. I didn't like it that she was playing with her.

At first, they were very surprised when they saw me, then they were very happy. F took me to get a bath but after my mother covered me with kisses and hugged me tight, she said that if the lawyers didn't give their permission, she couldn't let me stay the night because she'd signed a paper that very clearly said she wouldn't do that. Never in my life did I imagine I'd ever hear my mother say something like that. F got really mad and stormed out of the house.

As I was cleaning up, I realized Dania was wearing my flip-flops, my favorite skirt, and my brown jacket. I was furious.

Chela and the director tried to explain everything to my mom but she didn't understand. Just when they'd about convinced her, just as she was taking care of the cuts on my forehead, two social workers and a woman from the CDR walked in. They argued with us, they pulled out copies of the law and searched the house. They made quite a scene. At the end of it all, they put me in an olive-green Jeep in front of everyone and brought me here, to this school.

It was a heck of a trip. We got here around three in the morning. We're in a town called Cruces. My mother was crying when we left but I don't want to see her right now. I realize she's always been a coward, and so long as she's that way, we'll never be together.

They don't like it when this place is called an orphanage, so it's called a boarding school instead.

There's the sound of reveille. I'll continue tonight.

Saturday, January 12, 1980

"Justice can be exercised without intermediaries, without lawyers. Justice can be practiced by being just," the director of the group told my mother, the social workers, and the sleazy woman from the CDR. It was quite a speech, but it didn't make any difference. I wanted to write it down before I forgot it, but now I've got it stuck in my head and it won't go away.

There are visiting hours tomorrow but I don't want to see my mother. I already told the psychologist. I don't want to see her for a good long time. The psychologist asked me if I needed anything, and I told her I needed a notebook so I could write my Diary. They've given me the okay to write. I just have to be mindful of lights out.

The food here tastes like smoke; the milk tastes like smoke and it has a disgustingly thick skin on top. The omelets look burned, but at least I get to eat every day while I'm here. At home, unless F was around, nobody really cooked. Hours would go by and my mother would only brew coffee and make buttered toast. It was even worse with my father. Here I get stinky peas and watery stew, but it's food. You have to pick the weevils out of the rice, but at least that's entertaining.

There are two different sections at school. One is for reeducation, for the kids who've done something wrong and who are now being punished. That's on the other side of the fence.

The orphans and the kids abandoned at the hospital are on my side of the fence. There are also kids whose parents left the country and made no effort to reunite with them. Since they don't have family, they live here now.

They dress them nice on Sundays for the childless couples who visit, so they might get adopted. But many get visits from grandparents or aunts and uncles who can't take care of them full-time. The littler you are, the easier it is to get adopted.

Misuco, who bunks next to me, says that what she wants is to get to high school age so she can leave here and go to one of the country schools and even have a boyfriend. She doesn't want to be adopted. The psychologist explained to me that I won't be adopted, but there's nowhere else for me right now.

Since I haven't done anything wrong, I'm here until the lawyers say otherwise.

Cruces is the ugliest place I've ever seen in my life.

Sunday, January 13, 1980

My mother didn't come to see me.

The psychologist is a liar. They dressed me up in stiffly starched clothes that smelled of cockroaches, and they put me out on the line so that the childless couples could look me over. At least two of them singled me out. I'm sick of so many lies.

I was really embarrassed, though. A woman said I had to respond to all their questions. The kids there were really amazed by my story.

I don't want to write anymore. I hate Sundays, but not because of what happened. I've always hated Sundays, and now more so.

Monday, January 14, 1980

I'm being punished, but I don't know why.

Misuco came into my bed around dawn. She wanted me to be the woman while she played the man. She touched me for a while. Her fingers were so cold, they felt like a cat on my back. At first, I didn't understand what she wanted because I was half asleep. Then I got it. I pushed her away when she tugged at my underwear and wanted to stick her hand between my legs.

Then the lights flashed on and we were caught.

They think I'm involved in this, but I was merely asleep in my bed when Misuco fell out of the sky. I'm going to defend myself. I'm not going to be quiet. In just four days, I've come to realize there's too much going on in here. They say it's worse on the other side of the fence. I don't even want to know.

My punishment is to sit in the office. The cockroaches fly around me or walk up the walls, but I'm not afraid of them. They've been entertaining me since I lived with my grandparents on the Prado in Cienfuegos.

Tuesday, January 15, 1980

I'm not afraid to sleep here, nor am I afraid to be called a snitch. How could I be afraid of these girls after I fought with my father and got away?

They've calmed down now. I made a deal with the principal.

If they leave me alone, I won't tell on the teachers who sell cigarettes and weekend passes to the bigger kids. They actually proposed it to me, even though I'm nine years old, but now it turns out I have to stay for the adoption line. Of course they know I have parents who will come and get me. That's why they think they can sell me the weekend passes, because they think I have a place to go if I leave.

I'm not going to go home. I have to adjust to being here. My mother doesn't care one way or another if I ever go back to the lagoon. She's adopted Dania, as they say here during the morning sessions, and she doesn't want more trouble with the lawyers. I'm not even going to discuss my father.

I'd rather be here. I know in the end they're going to respect me. The kids are worse than the adults because they're not afraid of the consequences. But if I can deal with the adults, I can deal with the kids.

Thursday, January 17, 1980

A woman came and talked to me through the fence yesterday.

She brought me candy, but I know that it could be brujería so I threw it into the latrine. There are no toilets here, like in Escambray, just latrines, which are holes in the ground with wooden boards around them where you pee and shit. Once a week, I have to throw ashes in the holes to contain the stink. It was my turn today. It's truly disgusting; people throw all kinds of stuff down there. It looks like a kaleidoscope. Clothespins, sanitary napkins, ripped photos, cigarette packs, broken plastic doll arms. Everything winds up down there. (That's because after you clean up the patio during your shift, everything gets tossed down there instead of in the bonfire in the back.)

Well, this woman in a very pretty blue dress and heels showed up. She told the unit chief—one of the older girls, a redhead who's really nice—that she wanted to see me.

The woman told me about her life for a while. She lost a pair of twins in a car accident. It was so awful, I'm not going to retell the story. She said she knew I had parents, but that if they wouldn't take care of me, she could adopt me. She begged me not to decide until Sunday. I was mortified. I never imagined this could happen.

When she left, the redhead asked me how much the woman was going to pay me to let her adopt me. That really got me worried. The school keeps telling me I'm not adoptable, but the woman wants to adopt me. The redhead says they should pay me. I don't know what to do, and I can't ask my mom.

The redhead says she wants a cut of whatever I get. I asked her what it would be, more or less, and she said a hundred pesos.

One hundred pesos!

Saturday, January 19, 1980

My father came to see me on Sunday. The psychologist sat between him and me so she could hear the whole conversation. I refused to be alone with him. My father told me it'd be best if I went with him of my own free will, because he'll win again in court. I said no, I said no every time. The psychologist pleaded with him to leave, and I ran out so I wouldn't have to kiss him.

Fausto came later. They didn't even let him in since he's a foreigner, but I managed to see him through the back fence anyway. The redhead told me he'd be there. I owe that girl so many favors! Fausto said hi through the bars and gave me the little white feather, squeezing my hand really tight so I wouldn't lose it. He said he was leaving for Sweden Thursday night, and that he'd see us there before summer.

My mother must be winning the battle. Otherwise, Fausto wouldn't have said anything about meeting us in Sweden. Also, my father's been doing a lot of groveling lately. It must be for a reason.

NOTE

Fausto asked me to tell him what kind of food I'm being fed at school. I told him what I could remember from the last week. He wrote everything down, then he blew me a kiss and left in a car.

- Rice, boiled peas and fish, red beans, white pudding.
- Rice, peas, boiled egg, boiled plantain, rice pudding.
- Rice and beans, codfish fritter, boiled potato, rice pudding.
- In the morning, burned milk and a biscuit.

Sunday, January 20, 1980

I got into a fistfight with Misuco because she thinks she can tell all the girls in the home what to do, including me. But my mother says that only you tell can yourself what to do, and you can't lie about it.

We were in the showers, which aren't really showers but rusty pipes, and she told me to wash out her underwear. I didn't want to be her servant. Besides, the soap I use is the redhead's and I didn't want to waste it. Misuco said she'd wait for me outside. I just went ahead and hit her right there and then, before she could wait for me because then she'd catch me unawares and it would've been worse. She slipped and got a cut on her forehead. The doctor doesn't think it's serious since she didn't need stitches. She didn't tell on me, mostly because she's already afraid of me. She didn't even mention my name. There's a lot I could use against her. I don't write those things here because this is about what concerns me, not to snitch on anyone.

Thursday, January 24, 1980

My mother and Norma came to see me.

Norma is the woman who wants to adopt me. My mother was ashamed because she never imagined the school would ever ask her to come in to talk about such a thing.

"How can a girl with parents be put up for adoption?"

"Because it doesn't really look like she has parents," I muttered to her.

The teacher and the principal were stunned. My mother blushed. The principal began to giggle. Two days ago she had told me that given my parents and what they'd named me—Nieve means snow—I was bound to go crazy. It's nuts to name a child Nieve in Cuba, where it's so hot.

My mother's here now, with a document from the lawyers that lets her take me away from here. Norma takes us in her car, a little Polish auto that looks like a sardine can. I'm writing in the back seat. My mother doesn't dare say a word to me. I'm not even sure I want to go home anymore. The only person who said good-bye to me was the redhead, who is very nice and doesn't have anyone to get her out. I feel bad for her. Every time a door closes, it seems I'll never see the people behind it ever again. I stare at them so I won't forget them. It's a brief moment, but a moment in which I pack everything up into what I can see. I named those moments The Neveragains because I know I'll never again go back there, or there, or any of the other places I've lived.

I think we're going back to the high-rise apartment; enough of the lagoon. Fausto left this morning, so we would just be guests at the lagoon anyway. So much for the joys of going to the beach. There's no way to ever get used to any one place.

I'm curious what my mother will finally say to me when we're alone later today.

This car is really shaky. I'm closing my Diary.

Friday, January 25, 1980

Listen to what my mother's been saying: "She was one girl when she left, but she's come back another." I don't make the bed or help out around the house. She wants me to be how I was when I left. But I'm tired of putting up with all that.

She told me that Fausto was suddenly ordered to leave for Sweden. They gave him twenty-four hours to buy a ticket and get out. She says we have to whisper everything because they're suspicious of everything. Our plans to leave. Our plans to exchange the house for something in Havana before we get our permits to leave. Everything has to be planned out under terrible pressure.

Tomorrow, we'll go to Elpidia's beach with Leandro, a painter friend just back from art school who's going to live with us. My mother doesn't like it when we're alone. She says he'll get the housing exchange. But we have to be quiet about everything for now.

Sunday, January 27, 1980

First, we went to the train station.

Leandro showed up with quite the hairdo. I don't know what you call it, but it's big and round. Since he's mixed, it gets pretty frizzy. Leandro says he's not mixed, but he is.

Then we took our suitcases home. We didn't talk because we assumed we were being spied on. But as soon as we got to the beach around six o'clock, I found out what's going on. We talked with the water up to our necks. This is just how things are done at my house now. I'm going to make a list so I don't forget:

1) My mom says we'll see Fausto again real soon because my father's "not doing well," which means horribly, and he'll have to give his consent.

2) Leandro wanted to say good-bye to Fausto at the airport but he couldn't because Fausto was escorted by two soldiers and he couldn't get near him. I think he was some sort of prisoner.

3) It looks like Fausto wrote a letter to a child welfare organization, and that's why I was released from the orphanage.

4) Leandro managed to get us a house in Havana through an exchange, but who's going to hire my mother with so many problems?

5) A group of Leandro's friends arrive Sunday for an exhibition.
    It's the same people who came last year for "Fresh Paint." That
    means more problems for my mom, I know it.

Leandro's painting in the living room and he's made a huge
mess on the floor.

I have to go join my mother in bed now. I'm so sleepy. Until
tomorrow.

Tuesday, January 29, 1980

Leandro took a lot of pictures of me for his next exhibition. He saw me playing on Zero Avenue and took a whole series. When he thinks I'm talking too much, he says, "Hey, Nieve, make yourself scarce." And I do, immediately.

My favorite of his recipes is the one for Sprouted Chickpeas. You let them soak for several days until they sprout, then you cook them with salt, oil, tomato sauce, and garlic. You eat them cold. It's delicious.

Contrary to what they say at school, Leandro is not my mother's boyfriend. He gets up early, gives me my milk, and takes me to school without fail. He's a friend, that's all.

Thursday, January 31, 1980

My mother cried last night. Leandro went to the movies because he can't deal with the blackouts, so we were left by ourselves again. She promised that we'll see Fausto again, that we'll live in Stockholm, that my tummy will feel better, and that we'll put our lives back together.

"I promise, sweetheart, because I'm the master of your fate again, and everything will be different this time."

My mom is so foolish that she doesn't realize that no one is the master of their own fate here. She tells me lies, but not because she's trying to deceive me. It's because she wants us to be happy, and she tells them to lift my spirits. I think I'm slyer at nine than she is as an adult. Her problem right now is that she hasn't heard from Fausto. I'm sure that's it. We just have to be patient.

Leandro says they cut all the nude scenes out of the movie. Since he's a painter, he can tell. He was really mad about it.

I'm going to bed. There's no point in writing at this hour. I have classes early tomorrow.

Friday, February 1, 1980

Leandro and my mom's painter friends have arrived.

Since they couldn't get rooms at the San Carlos Hotel, they're staying here. They all have long hair and wear faded jeans. There's a really tall guy with green eyes and an actor's face who set up a tent on the roof.

There's no exhibition. We're going to an indigenous settlement. But we can't call it an indigenous settlement because Cuba had no Indians, just aboriginals, Taínos, and all that stuff they teach us in school. We're going to dig up wood and clay idols in the mud. Not gold or silver idols, no, because their civilization had very few of those and in Puerto Casilda there aren't that many.

We're going to Cayo Carenas today.

My mom shows everyone the wooden houses there and points out the Russian submarines in the water. They come up to the surface every now and again, but you're lucky if you spot any.

There's a young man who's very charming. He wears a beard and a camera swung around his neck. He takes photos nonstop.

There are about six painters altogether. The chubby one brought some new records. My mother's record player was broken but he fixed it. They're listening to a group that sings in English.

My mother stood up and declared that everyone knew what was and wasn't banned. She said that in the provinces it's illegal to even listen to the radio, and so everyone can do whatever they want in our apartment. People are going to talk anyway.

I'm going to be very entertained on this trip, but as soon as everyone goes back to Havana, we'll surely get a visit from the neighbor who always comes over to scold my mother and ask her annoying questions. She doesn't care. She says these things don't happen in Sweden. We're not doing anything wrong.

At Cayo Carenas

The first wooden house on this key belonged to my father's family. I hardly ever saw them because they didn't like my mother, and besides, they left a long time ago for the United States. The house is abandoned, and my father doesn't like to come here on vacation. Everything is in ruins. "It's criminal," my mother says.

There's an American engineer who lives here named Andy Simon. He wants to build a bridge to Pasacaballos, but everyone says he's crazy and they pay him no mind though he has the plans spread on his table. I like to arrive by boat and swim in the standing pools. Leandro found a chadka, which is a furry Russian hat. We haven't seen any submarines yet today.

Another one of the painters is a friend of Zaida's, the artist who always stays with us. He's short with almond eyes, quiet and very nice. He's the cutest of the bunch. He asked me to tell him the story of the flowers for Camilo. My mother's always telling my school stories after I go to bed, then I have to tell them again the next day.

The thing is, every October 28 since Camilo disappeared into the sea, the children go to the seawall in Cienfuegos and throw him flowers because if he's there, under the water, then he receives them. Last October 28, though, it rained so much we thought we were in for a hurricane. My teacher at Rafael Espinosa School, where I go when I'm in Cienfuegos, put a bucket in the middle of the room and told us to just throw our flowers there and that we'd march in a circle around it. Dania read the poem for Camilo wearing a broad-rimmed hat, and I read "Tengo" by Nicolás Guillén.

The painter just about died laughing and kept asking me to tell it again and again. Since I like to see him laughing, I told it two more times, then he called everyone over to hear it one more time. They just about drove me nuts.

Tuesday, February 5, 1980

We're in Puerto Casilda. Between all of us, we came up with three clay blades, two idols in pretty good shape, and one broken bowl. At night, we sang around the fire with some of the people who are doing excavations here.

The painters leave for Havana today. What a shame.

Last year's exhibition was more fun than what they've been working on these last few days. Not only did it feature paintings on the walls, but there was a TV, dried leaves on the ground, many photos, and a big guy who skated all over the gallery. Anyone who actually came in to see the paintings was shocked. My mother says the world changes and art changes with it. I think I'm going to study painting, but I'm not going to draw like my mother. I'd like to do something more like them. You can just tell by looking at them that they're artists.

We're on Marcos's pickup truck. He's the archaeologist in charge of the excavations. Everyone's asleep except my friend and me. He's the one who did the very large painting of Zaida lying on the grass. Maybe he'll paint me when I'm older. But even if he doesn't, I know we'll see each other again in Havana.

Thursday, March 20, 1980

I can't write, even in my Diary, because I'm trying to get up to speed at my new school. By my count, I've attended six different schools from preschool to now.

The teacher got mad because she wants me to write an essay about cartoons and I can't. I don't have a TV, my mom doesn't have the money to buy one, and even if she did, she wouldn't, because she says we have to read.

Dania gave me a list of Russian cartoons, and she's going to take me home with her so I can watch them. She says I don't have to let the teacher pick a fight with me just because I'm new. Dania goes to the same school we used to go to before.

Today is my mother's birthday. Spring begins tomorrow, and she wants to throw a party to celebrate the equinox. She says Fausto will call her in the wee hours to wish her a happy birthday. My father hasn't said anything about giving his consent.

We're not sure whether we should move to Havana or stay here.

Leandro is painting a mural on the Prado. They're paying him about three hundred pesos, but they made my mother go back to work at the radio station. She can't find another job. That's just how things are.

The same man who always comes to see her came again. I heard everything. He asked her about the painters, about Leandro, about Fausto, then he told her she could work at the radio station again, but he needs her to be less trouble this time.

My mother was disgusted. That was quite a birthday present. I bet she cancels the spring celebration.

Monday, March 24, 1980

We're working again at Radio City by the Sea.

My school's on the corner. I'm back at Rafael Espinosa School, the same as Dania. I stand up in class and say, "Who wants coffee or tea?" I jot down which students want tea and which teachers want coffee. Then I go over to the station and bring back whatever they want in little paper cups. It's just that I get so bored in my classes.

At five in the afternoon, I work with my mom on a children's program called *The Children's Circle*. Dania and I are the hosts. We read from scripts my mom writes for us. We talk about formal education, unidentified flying objects, and about Maceo, who is my mother's favorite national hero. We play music by María Elena Walsh and children's songs. I love working live. I always make a mistake or two, but my mom says it keeps the program fresh.

It's been a long time since we've heard from Fausto, and even longer since we've heard from my father.

Tuesday, April 1, 1980

They've closed down the radio station and they're just playing music, one song after the other. Someone wrote something inappropriate on the back wall.

My mother's indignant because they've asked me to write a few sentences, which she's sure is just a way for them to confirm my handwriting. It's not like I'm an adult who can come up with that kind of craziness.

This is what they had me write:

The stars twinkle up high.
Down below, everything's peaceful and Comandante Fidel
walks with confidence through the mountains of the Sierra Maestra.

They're plain wrong if they think it was me. I've got plenty of writing to do, just in my own Diary. They called me in but not Dania.

And who made me write that stuff out? The same man who comes over to our house to bother my mom.

My mother has asked for a medical excuse again. Now the radio station's over again.

Leandro got a job in Havana. He can't take this province anymore. He's going to work on a movie. He's doing the costume design. They're very pretty. I love how he paints on see-through paper.

We're alone again.

Just one more person who's left us.

Wednesday, April 2, 1980

My father came to see us. My mother says that at least he showed
his face.

He said that if he gives his consent, he'll get kicked out of the
Party, that he already has all kinds of problems because of what
happened with me. He came to explain himself and then left.

I don't get why he wants to be a member of the Party.

My mother offered him a cup of coffee because she's a fool. I
wouldn't have bothered with even a glass of water. When he tried
to talk to me, I just got serious and barely looked at him. He asked
about my grades, and I told him everything was going well.

My mother told him that it was probably best if he left, and he
did. When I heard the door slam downstairs, I thought: I am never
going to see him again.

My mother got very depressed after he left. She called Leandro,
who's already in Havana, and she told him that she'd never see
Fausto ever again. My mother can't leave unless I get my father's
permission to go with her.

At the very least, we have to move to Havana.

Leandro is going to help us.

Saturday, April 19, 1980

I'm writing while riding on the moving truck. My mother and I are riding up front. She had thought that what little we have could just stay in Cienfuegos, but in the end we carried it all with us. The Chinese vase my father left behind at the high-rise apartment is riding on her lap. It probably belonged to my grandmother, since she's the one in the family who had money.

I'm very curious because I've never laid eyes on Havana.

We have to start at the bottom, my mom says, so we're moving to a tenement. It's filthy and we'll have to clean it up. I'm not looking forward to this. Leandro is already there. He probably already cleaned up the place; he works harder than both of us put together.

I wonder how my new school will be. I'm so tired of being the new girl.

Havana's crazy. There's a parade going on by the Peruvian Embassy and we can't get through any of the streets. We're stuck at the Parque Central and the truck driver can't do a thing about our furniture.

My mother says a bunch of people crowded into the embassy so they could leave Cuba, even though they don't have permits.

"Are there a lot of people there?"

"Enough," she says.

Monday, April 28, 1980

I've been at my new school for one week. It's behind the Habana
Libre Hotel in Vedado. It gets lots of light and smells like the sweets
they make over at the hotel. It also smells like urine because they
never clean the bathrooms like they did in Cienfuegos.

The teachers are very nice and there are a lot of male teachers.
In Cienfuegos, there were hardly any men among the teachers. The
chalkboards look good: you can tell they're new. They gave me a lot
of notebooks—so many that I have enough for three more Diaries.
Now I come and go to school by myself because it's only four blocks
from home.

I don't know what I'm going to do. My mom has forbidden me
from attending the "acts of repudiation," the demonstrations they
hold when someone's leaving the country. I've seen them when I walk
around Vedado. People throw eggs, tomatoes, and rocks at the houses
of the people who are leaving. A little girl at school named Yazanam
calls those demonstrations "The Go-Gos." Sometimes they even drag
the people who are leaving on the ground. It terrifies me to think that
someone we know might want to leave. They remind me of my father:
beatings and beatings and you still can't go where you want to go.

The problem is that my mom doesn't understand that at school
they don't let you say no. They put you on a bus and send you off

to any of the Go-Gos going on somewhere in the city, which is so big and has more people leaving at any given time than anywhere else in the country. When I try to explain this to her, she just talks and talks and refuses to listen. She says it's inhumane, a violation of human rights. If I have to stay home and I can't sneak out at the time of the demonstration, my mom and I are sure to have a fight.

At school, they call me a peasant because I come from the provinces. But they're the peasants—they don't know how to pronounce words correctly. They swallow their S's and everything ends in "ele."

Tuesday, April 29, 1980

I sneaked out to a Go-Go sponsored by our school to comply with the requirement. I'm new and I don't want to have problems right off the bat. Nobody knows us here.

But I got pretty freaked out. They beat a man until they drew blood. His children were upstairs in the building with nothing to eat. Then they cut the water and gas. The man had come out to get food, and that's when they grabbed him. They've been beating him since dawn without rest.

If my mom finds out I'm here, she's going to kill me.

I didn't shout at anybody. I was just in my own head.

There are no classes again tomorrow because we have to go to another demonstration.

What do I do? Should I go or not?

Wednesday, April 30, 1980

I was standing in the park on the corner of H and 21st Streets. We had to shout: "Scum, lumpen, go, go! Go, go! Down with the worms!" It was all directed at a photographer who lives there. As soon as somebody said he was a photographer, I could picture him exactly. And like a fool I stayed.

He was a friend of my mom's.

She came by and saw me. She grabbed me up off the ground. Then she fell on her back and told me to look very carefully at everything around me. She was crying. She asked me if I'd taken a good look at everything that was going on so I'd never forget it. I said yes. And then, in front of everyone from my school, right in the park and without an ounce of fear, my mom screamed, "Let's leave this place. This is not what the revolution is about." I started crying because I thought they were going to yell at her.

My mom took my hand and directed us toward 23rd Street. I didn't even want to look at the teacher who'd brought us to the demonstration. My mother took me home and turned on the TV. They were showing the people inside the embassy. They were throwing food at them as if they were animals in the zoo.

We didn't say a single word about what was going on. Leandro was mute. Something happened, but I don't know what yet. I'll find out eventually.

The mashed potatoes were very good. Leandro added ham and a fried egg to them.

Thursday, May 1, 1980

Today is the March of the Combatants. My mother, Leandro, and I shut the apartment's only door and only window. This isn't an apartment but a single room with a loft and an unenclosed bathroom. We shut ourselves in and turned on the TV with the sound off. The TV belongs to a friend of Leandro's because we don't have one or the money to buy one.

From six in the morning there were knocks on the door, but we didn't answer.

They think we're at the march with people from school or work, so we can't make any noise. The old folks who stayed behind and didn't go to the march could find out we're still here.

All of a sudden, my mom saw a world-famous painter at the march. He is a little old man who looks Chinese; he's a friend of hers and of her art school professor. He was in a wheelchair, and his wife helped him cross in front of the tribunal.

My mom started crying again. Leandro turned off the TV.

When everyone came back from the march, we opened the window.

Friday, June 20, 1980

My mom sat with me up on the loft and finally told me what she'd had stuck in her throat for the last few days.

My dad snuck into the Peruvian Embassy so he could leave the country. My grandparents are waiting for him in Miami. My dad was in the first group that got in, so he must already be on his way.

I don't care. I told my mom this and she stayed quiet. As far as I'm concerned, it's for the best. He can't hit me anymore and now we don't have to wait for his consent to leave.

Leandro started to laugh. They hadn't thought of that. On Monday, we'll go and ask for our travel permits.

Monday, June 23, 1980

Today we took our documents to the office where you have to go to request a travel permit. We were in line a very long time. Everyone there is a soldier, and we were helped by a woman in an olive-green uniform. She asked my mom a lot of questions.

In the end, she offered my mother a tongue twister.

If my father left, it's because we want to leave too, for Miami.

If my father left and we're not headed to Miami, then he should have given us his consent.

But for my father to give his consent, he has to be in Cuba.

Since my father is not coming back to Cuba, I can't leave until I'm eighteen years old.

My mother didn't say anything. She left very quietly. She didn't shed a single tear. We went to a phone center so we could make a call. There we got into another enormous line. My mom talked to Fausto. "Forget me," was the only thing I heard her say. And then she hung up on him.

My mom shouldn't give up like that.

Wednesday, June 25, 1980

My mother is in the living room with the old painter she knows from art school, whose name is Lam. He came to see her with his wife, whose name is Lu and who is Chinese.

It's been a long time since I've seen my mother this happy. Lam is amazed by my mom's drawings and ceramics. She copies the aboriginals, but she can only do it when she's not working at the radio station. She can't dedicate her time to art the way she used to before I was born.

Lam also looked at my drawings and told me I'll be a great painter someday.

He invited my mom to France to help him with his ceramics studio in Paris. My mother said yes, but we all know that once he leaves they're not going to let us go. Exactly like what happened with Fausto.

I'm very sleepy. Lam painted a green emerald lizard with a palm tree, or something like that, in my Diary.

They invited Leandro too, and he'll be able to go. We're really going to miss Leandro. I don't know how we're going to manage all alone.

See you tomorrow.

The Adolescent Diary

We'll pass by the inferno of adolescence
as if on tenterhooks, because only
some poor devil would ever want to stop in hell.

—Eliseo Diego

Sunday, October 19, 1986

My mom says my generation loves gregariousness. She says we don't understand the I, just the We.

I imagine that's because we're their kids and they're the generation of May '68, the miniskirt, the gigantic mobilizations on those farm trucks for the sugar harvest, the park off the funeral home where they tattooed each other without anesthetic, the houses where fifteen kids would cram into one room to listen to the Beatles, who were more banned than meat. They're the pure products of the sixties.

Waldo Luis, my mother's best friend from art school, got shot for defending a dancer in La Pelota cafeteria at 12th and 23rd Streets. Some men showed up and pulled the trigger. Everyone brought flowers to the funeral. They sang in a chorus and read poems, and they still cry about him.

But we live somewhere between what's prohibited and what's required. We don't really have that spirit of solidarity they had back in the sixties. We live hiding in our bunk beds, the one thing we can all agree to love and respect. Sometimes we sleep two to a bunk, four altogether. Our wardrobes are community property. We lend each other clothing on the weekends. Nothing you bring to school is ever exclusively yours.

Food is swallowed quickly because we've never learned to savor anything in these semi-boarding schools we attend. We eat as if it was a relay race, living the slogan: "Whomever finishes first will help a comrade."

If you use silverware correctly you're called bourgeois, so it's better to just shovel it in with a spoon. We talk with our mouths full and use our index fingers to push food around. When I go home on the weekends, my mother calls me "the medieval pig farmer's daughter."

She doesn't get that you pay the price if you're different. They won't ever ask you out, not to concerts or the beach, or the parties that they throw just for fun. I've often found myself alone in those interminable lines to hear Silvio or Pablo sing while they have great fun in huge crowds, laughing it up, enjoying a happiness that's completely alien to me.

It's the cold war, the war of adolescent banishment. If you're not a part of the group, you don't have a boyfriend. If you're not popular, they reject you, they make fun of you, you're forgotten. You bother them, you're in their way, and that's why they retaliate. They can't stand that you have your own world, and I can't stand being rejected.

Nobody tells you you're pretty, that something looks good on you. Even when you're a part of the group, it's like there's an agreement I call "NO LOVE."

Literally, no love: If you love someone, even if you're together, you never say it. You make it a joke. Nobody takes responsibility for having such emotions. That's why relationships are so short. They last a month or two. There's always a misunderstanding because nobody ever says what they're really thinking. NO LOVE. If you tell somebody you love them, you're ostracized. NO LOVE. A guarantee then that you'll never hook up with anybody you actually like. To top things off, it's fashionable now not to kiss. They squeeze and touch each other, some people sleep together, but because it's all based on NO LOVE, they don't kiss. I don't understand any of it, but I'm surviving this circus anyhow.

I can't even imagine writing in my Diary in front of anybody at school. I'm always hiding my notebook because neither the students nor the teachers can see what I write here. It's possible that they would kick me out of school. The worst part of all of this is that we are art students. And even so, it's hard to be different.

Each one of us owes something to each martyr, according to my mother: Che's asthma, Camilo's body in the sea, the man who wrote Fidel's name in blood on a wall before dying, those who died in Angola, those who were lost in Bolivia, the warriors for independence—we owe everyone. They're the ones who did everything for us, and we can't do enough for them. I think we owed them everything before we were even born.

I owe my mother and that's it. As far as I'm concerned, the only martyrs are our parents. Sometimes we, the offspring, want to forget our surnames; we'd rather go through whatever changes to be just one more in the long line of students holding aluminum trays and waiting for lunch.

But I'm so sick of being just one more person singing along to the same stupid songs. I know it's just adolescence, but I shaved my head because I want them to know I'm me. I did it just this Saturday, leaving only a little bit up front and on the sides.

I know it's adolescence. I know that everything seems about to start but won't. In fact, it's really going to fall apart. It'll shatter into pieces like the Chinese vase that fell out of my mom's hands when she saw what I'd done to my hair. It broke. It just toppled from her hands when she saw me; because of my difference, blood flows in this fake dynasty. My mother got a cut on her finger from a piece of porcelain. Chinese vase, Chinese porcelain, my life written out in Chinese and I don't understand.

I'm not Chinese but I have different features that no one dares to explain.

That vase was all that was left of my paternal grandparents in my house. We swept it up and threw it in the trash. It'll disappear, taking my name with it, detaching me from everyone that's been attached to me in the past. "The bad has gone," my mother said. She kissed my forehead and put a Band-Aid on her finger so the blood wouldn't stain the uniform she's mending for the umpteenth time.

For my mom, nothing's unusual. In her mind, everything can be figured out. That's why we're together. That's why we never run out of things to talk about. She always finds a way out of a jam. There's no way to get angry with her—she's a champ. The martyrs are all dead but she's still alive, in spite of the bad news, in spite of the life she leads in this tenement full of marginalized people who fight at all hours.

Someday, I'll get her out of here. I know I will.

On the Bus to the Art School

I hate Sundays. I hate going back to school.

The sea of uniforms hits its zenith on Sundays at 7:00 p.m., and then there's the journey back to school with my classmates screaming and telling stories that sound awfully similar to last week's.

They're the good guys and I'm the bad girl, the black sheep's daughter. They sneak off to smoke stuff that's been smoked openly in my house since I was a child and never interested me. It's nothing new to me.

I don't want to be a hippie like my mother, I don't want Peace and Love. I want to be me. I don't think getting high is necessary. I'm fifteen years old.

They'll never accept me. They want me to act like my mother. She accepts everything, smiles, and never cares one whit about sharing whatever she has with whomever and bringing a whole platoon of people home with her to eat my food, people who'll judge me over and over. I'm me.

The leader here is Alan Gutiérrez. He does graffiti up on the little beach on 16th Street. I've already told him: I don't need to be a rebel to prove that I didn't spring from a manufacturing mold. His father is a hyperrealist painter, but Alan doesn't want to sell anything. His life is going in exactly the opposite direction from his parents. His family isn't having financial problems—he's at the boarding school in the country just because he wants to get away from his house, from schedules, from the family's friends. That much we have in common. Hanging out with Alan, I've written a few things on the wall at Colón Cemetery, at the little beach on 16th Street, and on Galiano, Monte, and Sitios Streets. I don't want to be a part of Arte Calle, his group. They don't accept women, and anyway he says I'm a coward. In all honesty, I have no interest in being brave. I'm taking a break from bravery.

I don't want to sketch the city anymore. The city's different now, with so much olive green and so many crumbling balconies. There are so many billboards and slogans, so many commands coming down on us from political posters. I don't want to hear one more decree. Now Alan wants to order me around. I'm not having any of it. Not one more command, not another man telling me what to do.

The most beautiful moment I shared with Alan was when we had a swap—his Mafalda T-shirt for my knit sweater. I was nude for a few minutes, and so was he. We looked at each other and dressed in silence. Neither of us touched the other. It was simply a gift. A pact, a ritual. I've never cared about being nude, but boys are different.

I brought home locks of hair from my cut yesterday because I want to make art with them. I've put two pictures of myself in the student photo gallery, one with long hair and the other with my hair short. The locks flutter, like black grass. I don't look like anyone else. If they read this Diary, they'd hate me.

Sometimes I think I'd like to blow up the pages of my Diary and exhibit some of them in the gallery. The school is made of red bricks, but in here, they're white. I'd love to write my ideas all over them. I've also thought about using neon for the letters, so they'd look as if they were written with fire or gold. But the power's always out at school...

My mother would die of fear. I quote her verbatim in my Diaries; she can't say in public what I have her saying here. Because of what I write, I hide my Diaries in the loft at home, under the boards. The humidity destroys them, but I copy over the letters with blue ink and I don't write every day in the new notebooks so they'll last a while. I have one started at school. I go everywhere with it. I bring it home, hidden between my other notebooks. My Diary is a luxury; it's my medicine, what keeps me standing. Without it, I wouldn't live to see twenty. I'm it, it's me. We're both wary.

Wednesday, October 22, 1986

My mother also went to this school. She was in the first visual arts class that inaugurated it in 1962. Because I look so much like her, some of the older teachers recognize right away that I'm her daughter.

She came from a little town called Banes, but since the hospital she was born in was in Guantánamo, where there's an American military base, she had dual citizenship. But she had to renounce it when she came to school. "Here, being an American is worse than being a leper," she said. When her parents chose to leave for Miami, she wanted to stay in Cuba and so they erased her from their lives. She remained alone in Cuba, where they made her a "child of the nation." She had no weekend passes or New Year's Eves away from school because she didn't know anyone in Havana. Sometimes her friends from the city would invite her out for a stroll, but she knows the labyrinths of the old country club where the art school is located much better than she does the actual city of Havana.

The school is very beautiful. There are enormous trees throughout the campus, and if you gaze down at it from above, from the lookout point, it's shaped like a naked woman built from red refractory bricks. Right now, I'm sitting at the fountain, which is where her sex would be, and the water flows all the way to my feet as

I write. It was designed by three architects: two Italians and one Cuban, Porro. He also left many years ago, and he writes to my mom at the end of each year.

She told me that since she was stuck here on weekends, she'd run into the architects while she painted. She'd go up to the lookout with them and they would tell her about the circus school, which was never finished, and about how this labyrinthine world would turn out once they completed it. They had a great time together.

One Saturday, my mom had to finish a homework assignment, but since she didn't have a model, she went to the far end of the campus, close to where the rich people had once lived and where now only their abandoned houses remained. She took off her uniform top, placed a piece of mirror on the easel, unfolded a piece of paper and began to draw her own torso. Out of nowhere, a Jeep approached. Because she's so audacious, she just kept working as if the visit had nothing to do with her.

The man who got out of the Jeep turned out to be Che. He was alone and, according to my mom, he asked about four hundred questions. She answered a few but never stopped working. Within about ten minutes, the principal and all the students who'd stayed for weekend guard duty showed up to watch the scene. My mom, her torso nude, continued talking with him as she painted.

When he left, they wanted to punish her in about a thousand different ways for being nude on the former golf course, especially since she was not a model, and in front of Comandante Ernesto Guevara. But because the worst punishment was always canceling the weekend passes and my mom never got one anyway, they just harassed and threatened her until they got tired and left her alone.

My mom says Che was a man like any other, that there was nothing out of the ordinary about him. Everyone asks her if she was impressed by him, and she always says no, that he was nice and normal. She doesn't like exaggerations.

If I don't hurry, they're going to close the dining hall. I'm going to have to sleep on an empty stomach.

Tuesday, October 28, 1986

Today they're taking us to a military training camp.

Since we can't ruin our hands working in the fields because we're the artistic future of the nation, they've decided to swap out the required 145 school days doing farm work for the same number of days at the School of Military Preparation. They don't want what happened to Andrés to happen to anyone else. He was a cellist who tore a tendon working in the fields.

I hate all things military—even the camouflage pants that are so trendy right now—but if I don't go, they'll kick me out of school. As the slogan says, "Every Cuban should know how to shoot, and how to shoot well." I wasn't born to shoot guns.

My mom and I made a deal. I brought a little transistor radio with me and I left her a list of my favorite songs. She'll play them when she can on her programs on Havana City Radio. She didn't let me list any songs in English because she can only play two of those a day. She says that's called "musical politics."

I've never had a firearm in my hands before. I can't imagine someone like me shooting at a target. My mother says it's illegal to arm adolescents. My mom will never be satisfied. She really doesn't get it. She asked me not to go. She still thinks about leaving the country, but who's going to claim us from abroad? Who's going to take us on at this point in time? We've never again heard from my father. Fausto remarried. Everything depends on just the two of us. So I have to go, and here I am, on the bus and about to learn how to use a machine gun.

We left on Monday and we'll return Friday. At least I can go home. If I were doing farm work, I wouldn't be able to go home for 145 days.

We're on a bus with the musicians. It's so noisy, my God. Everybody's brought their instruments so they can practice. This bodes well.

Wednesday, October 29, 1986

We still haven't laid eyes on any firearms. We copy crazy stuff like this over and over. I don't know if it's science fiction or if we'll ever get to practice with real guns. I only write down some parts of what they dictate to us. My mother will freak out when she reads this.

ORIGINAL VALERO MORTAR SHELL, 50 mm

It's made up of:

- An egg-shaped shell divided into two parts that fit together, encircled by a brass ring independent from the shell.
- A stabilizer, which is a hollow cylinder screwed to the grenade shell. The back part contains six stabilizing panels, and there are various openings in the front to disperse the fire from the propellant cartridge.
- 125 grams of gun powder.

The original grenade has an opening at the bottom to introduce the blasting cap that locks in the gun powder. There's a spring that presses down to propel it. Once outside the propelling cannon, the compressed black powder goes off.

HAND GRENADE

Procedure: Take the safety off the lock, throw the grenade. In theory (it's a lot to theorize), the weight of the grenade top will make the end of the fuse hit the bottom of the grenade, causing the spring to move the hammer, hitting or (as the ancient manuals say) beating the piston that ignites the explosive reaction.

There are some samples from Teruel (from the battle of the same name).

This particular grenade is also known as a *chinito*, because of the peculiar shape of its fuse, which looks like the kind of hat worn in those latitudes.

As to handling it, if the grenade is more or less in good condition, great care must be taken because the explosive it's filled with is extremely unstable. With its also extremely sensitive fuse, it's considered very dangerous.

For example, I can say that the explosive, in at least one case, exploded from just being touched by a screwdriver that was being used to extract it.

TECHNICAL CHARACTERISTICS:

• Width: 56.5 millimeters.

• Length: approximately 325 millimeters.

• Weight: ?

• Fuse: "for impact"

• Explosive: ?

• Materials: wooden handle and metallic shell.

What I want to know is: Why do we have to write all this down? What do I care about how to activate a grenade so I can kill and acquire what I don't want? We should also have the option of losing. I'd like to be a loser if my only other option is to shoot and hurt someone. I don't think my aim is good enough to kill anyone. To fight or not to fight. I imagine that's not the question at hand right now. This is a simple simulation.

I came fully equipped with books. They're the only things I brought. I can't stand to march in the evenings; it's best not to even talk about the food. Compared to this, the food they serve at school is a luxury.

I have to be careful when they finally give us the firearms: I'm about to shoot myself.

The sea is in back of the camp. This city is right on the water. I breathe deep and I can feel the salt in my nose. I feel better knowing I can swim out somewhere. Where, I don't know, but I'll go swimming forever someday.

At eight o'clock in the evening, my friend Mauricio, the journalist and announcer who works with my mother, said my name on *Good Night, City*. He played the Spinetta song I like the most: "Muchacha (Ojos de papel)"; they also sent me a kiss.

They dedicated the song to me; my mother has kept her word on the first day of the agreement. I almost died laughing because she said I should take it easy, but it also made me sentimental. There's a silly tear hanging off my chin. Life is over there, at the radio station, while we're fenced in here, learning to kill someone we don't even know yet.

"Muchacha (Ojos de papel)" ["Girl (Eyes of paper)"]
by Luis Alberto Spinetta

And don't talk, girl
with a heart of chalk,
when everyone sleeps
I'll steal away a color.
Girl, a sparrow's cry,

where are you going,
stay until morning.

Thursday, October 30, 1986

We got up at six and went marching without breakfast. We finally met Lieutenant Rolando, a mixed-race man who's in charge of the girls' group. He threatened us, told us disgusting jokes; he basically decided his tactic with us would be indecency. He made it clear as day that the girls' platoon is his favorite. He said that here we'll really prove that men and women are equal, but since I've never believed in that kind of equality, and much less in women's liberation, I didn't pay much attention to him. According to my mother, women's liberation is canned food so we can get out of the kitchen as quickly as possible, a good electric washing machine so we can get laundry done without too much effort, and the rest you figure out for yourself. In our case, we are not yet liberated.

The lieutenant made us march for four hours straight. Then we had lunch and, finally, they took us for target practice at the "dog's teeth," which is what they call the rocks on the shore. My thighs and elbows are scratched, my olive-green pants are torn, and my eyes hurt from staring through the sight I could never center quite right. My aim is awful. The guns are very heavy and I think the bullets are blanks. The smell of smoke makes me nervous.

After taking a shower, I tried to lie down and read in peace, but they made me go to the dining hall. I'm not hungry but I have to go. This is a military regiment, after all. Orders must be obeyed. Personal desires must stay packed up at home, in a locked box. Here, we're bound to fulfill the wishes and whims of others, supposedly our superiors, who want to compete with women and whatever other sensitive creatures happen to be around, all for the good of the nation and to kill an enemy who doesn't exist. Our olive-green uniforms confuse things. I don't know who's who anymore. I'm the only one—with my short hair—who sticks out in this uniformed sea.

Since I was a kid, I've asked myself why our president is the only one in the world who wears olive green. When I was thirteen years old, my mother explained to me that there used to be a new president approximately every four years. She was horrified when I told her I thought presidents died like kings, to be replaced by their children or siblings, and that their families would continue to govern eternally, enduring in tradition just like the national seal, the flag, and the national anthem.

I don't know why I find olive green such an odd color. None of my classmates are bothered by being here. I'm such a weirdo. Why do I insist on being different?

I'm off to the dining hall, marching.

NOTE

Something curious happened on my mother's radio show tonight.

They'd invited the singer-songwriter Carlos Varela. Mauricio interviewed him. Then he sang a new song, but he never came back on again, and they played prerecorded music the rest of the time: Silvio and Pablo. Strange. Anyway, I was able to copy part of Carlos's song, which is marvelous:

I barely open my eyes
and all the silence vanishes.
With breakfast
I swallow the noise and smoke
of the city.

I'm barely out the door
when someone starts to complain,
putting my wishes into words,
he says it's already been too long
and on the corner there's a sign
that says: Freedom;
that's my truth.

I'm starting to find myself,

as I run across the street

and lose myself among the people

wanting to dream,

everyday things make me dream.

I barely open my eyes.

Friday, October 31, 1986

I read, I write, I march, I shout slogans, I salute with my hand on my forehead, and, when I can, I rest.

Orders, orders, orders.

Yes, my lieutenant; yes, my lieutenant; yes, my lieutenant. I don't know why we have to say "my," but he demands it.

For the lieutenant, everything we do is toward one goal only: to kill "the enemy." I don't know who this opponent is, but the moment will come when we meet him. The lieutenant says we'll be ninjas by the time we leave this place.

I'm trying to be just one more in the crowd. If that lieutenant decides to pick on me, I'm dead. He's already chosen a few girls from the platoon to be his punching bags—poor things—and I really feel for them. The thing is, the lieutenant likes big, curvy women and I'm just a girl—and with this short hair, I look more like a boy. I don't think he's going to bother with making me shoot more, nor put up more targets for me to shoot at. He likes to harass the tall blondes from Music and Dance. He's very concerned with impressing them with his great aim.

Today, while I was waiting for the truck to take me to the firing range for class, one of those poor blond girls came up to me. She's so white she's translucent. Her nails are bitten down to the quick.

The bags under her eyes are purple and she shakes when she talks. She's a violinist, and it's easy to see that she's been studying for years without expressing herself much. The girl told me she sees me reading every day and wants to tell me something.

We went behind the laundry room to talk. She didn't want to talk in front of anybody, and less so in the barracks. She was being pretty mysterious. The blond girl's name is Lucía. She said that since she saw me reading all the time she wanted to ask me a question. She repeated this about a thousand times. She said her grandfather was a Cuban writer. I was happy when she told me this, but she was clearly frightened when she said, abruptly, that the writer had left the country about two years before we were even born. At the end of the seventies. She's only seen him in photos.

Ángel López Durán is Lucía's grandfather.

"But isn't he a homosexual?" I asked, worriedly.

Terrified, Lucía denied it and, asking me to lower my voice, she put her ice-cold hands over my mouth.

Suddenly, we heard the noise of the bus arriving. Quickly, she begged me to lend her any books of his that I might have, but I've never read her grandfather's work. Her father is a military man, and they don't talk about any of this at home.

I told her my mother probably has one of his books.

As we ran to catch the bus, we realized it was a truck instead. We climbed on together, helping each other. A very fine rain began to fall. Then it got more intense and everyone began to sing with an incredible joy. Some dirty see-through nylon tarps appeared out of nowhere so we could cover ourselves. In the midst of the noise and the rain that was hitting our faces, Lucía shouted at me, "Don't tell anyone about my grandfather, not even your parents!"

She has no idea how many secrets I've kept to date. We did our target practice in the rain.

Wrapped in nylon, we looked more like replicants than soldiers. Lucía didn't hit a single can all damned afternoon. She trembled like she had a fever and the sight never neared the target.

We're going home today, but on trucks again. It's raining very hard.

I write as I wait for them to come get us. I hide the Diary from the lieutenant, who's getting soaked for no reason whatsoever, checking out the guns and the girls. What an unpleasant man.

And there's Lucía, trying to protect her violin by wrapping it in a plastic bag. She's pale and has an absent look.

The trucks are late. A few of the musicians are playing; everyone's on their own. The music sounds crazy, but it's not. I have no instrument to take care of. I am my own instrument. I am in and out of tune. Everything depends on what I manage to do in circumstances as different as they are strange. My throat hurts. I have to gargle with salt water as soon as I get back to Havana. I am my own nurse, my own cook, my own hair stylist, my own psychologist, my own...

The lieutenant smacked me on the butt and pushed me just as I was climbing on the truck.

Saturday, November 1, 1986

Drama, drama, and more drama. How we love and take comfort in drama.

My mother scares me when she cries like that. She can only hear censored stories. When I told her about the lieutenant, the downpour, and, lastly, the butt smacking, she almost died of shame.

I changed the subject and asked her about López Durán. I wanted to know if he was really homosexual because what confuses me is that Lucía said she's his granddaughter. My mom went from crying to hysterical laughter. It turns out that I'm confusing two great writers in exile, and she let loose with her favorite phrase about me: "You can put together an encyclopedia with what my daughter doesn't know."

She says that López Durán was sent as a Cuban cultural attaché to Europe at the end of the sixties, and he stayed (everybody in the world leaves). He then wrote some really tough novels about the problems in Cuba. His novels are banned here. If they catch you with one of his books, you're in big trouble.

My mom climbed up on the little wooden ladder. For the first time ever, I noticed her legs: they're beautifully, wonderfully shaped—feminine, nice. Her legs are her best feature. She's like the acrobat in Picasso's painting, always looking for balance with the only thing she has: her two strong legs to support her.

Behind all the books we can see there's another, well-hidden group. She began to pull out a handful of dusty volumes wrapped in colored paper. I saw three different books by López Durán, all excellent in her "modest" opinion. My mom said I could lend any of them to his granddaughter but to be careful, to not even think about taking any of them with me back to the military training camp because there'd be no saving us if I was caught.

I'll spend the weekend reading them. I want to know who Lucía's grandfather is. My God, so much drama!

Sunday, November 2, 1986

Carlos Varela has been banned from the radio because of the song he debuted on my mother's show. Apparently, the way he said "freedom" was problematic. I had realized immediately that something had gone wrong because of the way they'd cut him off.

If that had happened at the radio station in Cienfuegos, it would have been Varela and my mother who'd have hell to pay.

But what a pretty song. I think he studies scenic arts at the Institute of Art, right next to my school, but I don't know who he is. I'd love to meet him. My mother says he dresses in black and has very large, expressive eyes. He writes pure poetry. For her, it's an honor to take the risk of playing him, but they have to be careful for a while. She'll try again in a month and see how it goes.

BANNED FROM THE RADIO

Moncho

Raphael

Julio Iglesias

Celia Cruz

La Lupe

Olga Guillot

Miami Sound Machine

certain songs by Carlos Varela

Mike Porcel

Meme Solís

Willy Chirino

José Feliciano

Monday, November 3, 1986

As I was headed back to the military camp yesterday, I realized I already had many reasons to hate this day of the week, especially this violet hour. By seven o'clock there's no power, and if by chance there is power, they put on a program featuring the worst kind of country music. The sound echoes off the walls of the city as Havana's sepia lamps light up. That's when I know it'll be another week before I see those streets again, my friends from the radio station, my school, my mother, the world…our tiny world gets put away for several days.

When the first cold fronts reach Havana, all the girls come back wrapped in multicolored ponchos, coats knitted by their grandmothers, and borrowed sweaters.

Winter's here: a carnival for the poor.

When I got to the barracks, I got quite a surprise. Lucía was already there, asleep in my bed. I woke her and she asked me about her grandfather. She made me laugh; it was like she expected me to show up with her grandfather in my bag. I opened it and, without hesitation, I lent her the first of the three books that my mom has. I explained that if we got caught, we could wind up in jail. Lucía nodded and nervously climbed up to the bunk above me. She had traded with a neighbor so we could be together.

It's Monday, very early. I left so I could wash up and do some laundry, but when I came back I could see Lucía had not slept. She looks like a little white mouse reading her grandfather's book on the bed. She's practically holding her breath, drinking up the whole book, and I have no idea how she's going to deal with training today. The only thing she's said is that the whole family's in the novel.

It's obvious she hasn't slept, and that she's been crying.

Tuesday, November 4, 1986

If everything I read in López Durán's novel really happened to Lucía's family, then poor girl. Of course, everyone here has a story, and if not, they can ask my mom, who was abandoned on this island as a "child of the nation."

Lucía's still stretched out on the upper bunk. She said she was dizzy and had aches and pains all over her body so she could skip training and finish the rest of the book. The lieutenant has come by to see her twice today. They'll catch her reading "that" at any moment and I'm going to have to leave the country. I've begged her to go to sleep and put the book away, but it's ten thirty at night and she's too stubborn to stop.

I'm sick of marching; even my soul hurts. My sore throat comes and goes.

I heard Mauricio talk on the radio about an exhibition called *Puré expone*. It was in January of this year, and I loved that show. People call in to give their opinions, but I know it's all taped: they can't have people talk openly like that, without censorship. I know the radio like I know the back of my hand. My mother must have made a deal with the wind because what's on the radio disappears in the air. When we lived in Cienfuegos, nobody could hear us three towns away. Now that we live in Havana, nobody can hear us in Cienfuegos. The station is just for the listeners who live in the city. Whatever happens stays right there, on the modulated frequency. I don't know why they worry so much about what goes on inside that little black box, since in the end the voices are lost and everything's gone with the wind.

We get letters at the radio station with pubic hairs and lipstick marks. Girls wait for the announcers at the door and are always disappointed when they see them. One day, a woman called the program and said, "Oh, Mauricio, I've had such a terrible day." And he said, "Well, just take a hot bath and listen to this record I'm going to play for you."

It's true that the radio helps people who are alone. It creates a fantasy world in the midst of this hard reality we're living. Mauricio makes it seem like it's very glamorous to be in the announcer's box, that they have a privileged view of the city, when in fact they work in a little chicken coop that's completely enclosed with no view whatsoever, not even of the street. Mauricio plays a game in which he says he has a flashlight and he signals people in other buildings with it, and they respond. But it's all in his head because he's in a sealed black box that's in my bed now, because radio is about illusion. Everyone believes what's said on the radio, except those of us who are children of the radio. Mauricio and I have a lot in common, but my mother won't let me so much as look at him. My mom says he'll go far because he's talented and works nonstop.

Tonight he dedicated "Eclipse of the Sea" by Joaquín Sabina and Luis Eduardo Aute to a nameless "little person." I don't know if it's actually for me, but that's the best part of the radio: even if I'm not at home, even if none of this is for me, I can make it mine and have it keep me company.

"Eclipse of the Sea"

about this eclipse of the sea, about this mortal leap,
about your voice trembling on the answering machine,
about the blanks that oblivion transmits a bed.
There's no talk about you in the paper, or about me.

Thank you, Mauricio. I hope the lights don't go out while I'm trying to write out these lyrics and thinking of you. Havana has its eras, each correlated to a song. That's how I see it and feel it. That's why I include them in my Diary, so they won't leave me.

The lieutenant is doing a whole lot of screaming at the barracks door. I close my Diary. I hear a man's voice. I turn off the radio.

Wednesday, November 5, 1986

It's very early and I haven't slept a wink. The city is empty. There are very few cars in the tunnel at dawn on the way back to Havana.

Last night was very sad. They burned López Durán's book in front of everyone.

Lucía defied Lieutenant Rolando and she got quite a beating in the office. It was just her and the lieutenant in there, and there was nothing anyone could do. Things have gone badly. Lucía seemed so flighty, but she defended herself as if she had actual claws. We've both been expelled from the military camp. Her parents are taking me home. What happened last night is such a long story that I don't know where to start. It feels like Lucía is going to die; we have to stop every five minutes so she can vomit. Her mother cries more than she does. Her father doesn't say a word. The situation is complicated because her father is a colonel.

I'm going home without my radio or the López Durán book. My mom will say she warned me and she won't hear any of the versions of the story I've prepared to defend myself. She'll say I'm a snob for lending out a book I hadn't even finished. She warned me a thousand times not to take that book with me to camp.

That lieutenant is a beast. Lucía has bruises everywhere. We're finally free of the military, but our problems have just begun.

Sunday, December 28, 1986

Disciplinary Council, Three Cases

A music student and two visual art students are before the Disciplinary Council of the National School of Art.

The three of us, what a coincidence.

Alan didn't go to military training. He stayed behind, painting at the school. Leave Alan Gutiérrez alone with a blank wall and wait and see what happens. The council is pretty severe. It's made up of the most mediocre, and most dangerous, professors at school. They're the only ones who volunteer for this kind of thing.

Lucía and I were sent home the same night the lieutenant discovered the transistor radio and the López Durán novel in the same bunk. I haven't had enough peace of mind to write again. It's been a real nightmare.

We accepted being judged by this Disciplinary Council because our only other option was to sign off on certain expulsion from school.

Alan painted his idea on the wall, the same idea he's always had: "Reviva la revolu"—which, he says, means to revive what has died, and more precisely, to reanimate what has not been completed. We each turned seventeen, one right after the other. They already treat us like adults, and they're not going to forgive us. We're too vulnerable. Too young to be judged, too grown to be pardoned.

I'm terrified. I get panicky thinking they'll send us off to a school like the one in Cruces, the kind that reforms adolescents. Alan and Lucía have no idea what that could mean. It's best to live without too much knowledge of what could happen to you. Although for Alan, this is perfect: he loves everything that's banned, he loves to take risks. His best experiences have been at the police station. Of course, he has someone who goes and stands up for him. I'm a "corpse without a mourner," as my mother says.

So I'm here again, in court. I should be used to it but I'm not; I know all too well what the consequences are. I can't smoke, like Alan, to calm my nerves, and I can't go cry in corners, like Lucía. I'm better off with my Diary: I just let go and get everything off my chest.

My mom didn't even bother to show up. She doesn't like this sort of thing. She says whatever trouble I get into because I disobeyed her is trouble I have to get myself out of. Lucía's parents are in the office and Alan's father is waiting in the car (he's always stylish, sweet, and gentle, reading something as if he couldn't care less if the world is about to end). I don't know whether I should say anything to him. Here he comes.

I can go on now.

Alan is a hero.

Even if he wants to order me around, even if he raises his voice at me, even if he's the only one who ever makes me cry, he is most definitely our hero and there's no point now in pretending otherwise.

Simply put, all three of us are guilty, each of our own misdeed. Lucía couldn't defend herself because she never said I'd lent her the book. My sin was listening to the radio while at a military barracks. And Alan was in the worst situation, because his mistake came under the category of "ideo-aesthetic" issues. He also knows that not one of those mediocre teachers on the council can deal with his macabre little mind.

First, we heard Lucía's mother confess that López Durán was her father, and that Lucía had simply been the victim of normal adolescent curiosity about the past. Then Lucía's father said that for him, as a military man, it was disappointing to see his daughter "unearth that cadaver."

After all that, I was ready to be burned at the stake because I figured Lucía would say I was the book's owner. They'd made her sick with the question from day one. I have nothing to lose if she tells, except school. My mother is not going to judge me in the same way as Lucía's father, who is an ogre and who hasn't even mentioned that she was beaten.

It had already been established that the lieutenant had hit Lucía, but when Alan finished with his defense he incriminated the lieutenant even more.

Alan began by talking about his work, repeating a phrase that he always uses in theoretical discussions: "The most important thing is the idea, and that justifies the means." That's why, he says, he paints walls arguing that the revolution has not been completed. Then, mixing everything into the same pot, he said Lucía hadn't wanted to speak openly about her mistreatment at the hands of the lieutenant who not only hit her, but also wanted to rape her. Lucía was terrified, and then he gave her one of his intimidating looks. I know all too well Alan's classic repertory of looks. That was look #22, the intimidating punisher.

Lucía became so frightened she began to cry. Alan said her problem was how not to stain the "olive green," because it was the same "olive green" as her father's uniform. According to Alan, she was keeping all her pain to herself and only had the strength to confess it to him in a moment of weakness just before we came before the council.

When he spoke about me, he said that I had an attachment to the radio because my mother always sends me encouraging messages on her programs and he confirmed that I was caught listening at the same time that *Good Night, City*, the show she writes and produces, is aired.

We were pretty astounded by Alan. What did he know about my mother's programs, or radio broadcasting schedules, or even my emotional needs? I couldn't imagine him ever listening to those shows, which a guy like him would likely have considered a "lesser art."

Then he came back to the themes of his work and went head-first into postmodernism. "Postmodernism is the best sign of capitalism's decay," he testified. Then he added: "The day my ideas cease to be revolutionary is the day I'll have reason to fear." Nobody understood much of it, but the professors left to deliberate in admiration. I know very well that he uses the concepts of revolution and postmodernity very differently than the professors but, in the end, it's another great misunderstanding—this one in our favor.

Communication Breakdown

Coherence breaks down when you have to make things up to defend yourself. As if reality wasn't enough. We had no choice but to blend fact and fiction. After all, that's how we were raised: hiding our books, our ideas, our relatives. At this point in the game, what does it matter if we lie or manipulate the truth? A man who beats a woman is also capable of raping her. Someone like the lieutenant can be a real monster. And as Alan would say, "Where's the enemy then?" Is the enemy Lucía's grandfather, who writes books we're not allowed to read, or Lieutenant Rolando, who vents his violence on us?

"Where is the enemy?"

Everyone applauded. All three of us were absolved, with a hell of a warning on our school records. Nonetheless, it doesn't matter: those records are worthless and someday they'll get tired of reading them. Someday, they'll burn them in a pyre like they did my mother's in the yard at the old country club, which is now this school, and which tomorrow will be God-knows-what.

When I heard Alan defend Lucía, I realized there's always a guy, in every group, in every decade, in every place in the world, who'll come to a woman's rescue in the nick of time. Some will be heroes and some will be martyrs: Waldo Luis, my mother's friend, died in the middle of the street the winter of 1970 because someone tried to stop him from defending a dancer from his class. And now Alan told this story, practically immolating himself for the two of us—though, in fact, his problem got mixed up with ours—and all of us came out clean because of the wide path he opened up with his particular jargon.

Lie or truth, I don't know.

Alan, Lucía, and I went to the boys' bathroom to talk among ourselves before the verdict came in. Neither the stench of the bathroom nor the amateur graffiti on the walls could distract us from the matter at hand. It was funny. The whole time, Alan kept asking Lucía if she'd liked her grandfather's book after all. Lucía wept and laughed. Alan smoked nonstop. He didn't even look at me.

When they announced the decision, he kissed me on the mouth—right in front of the teachers and parents. I almost died of shame; I thought his mouth would never come off mine. This was the first real kiss I'd received in my whole life; the others didn't count at all. It was practically my first kiss ever, and it happened without my understanding it. How can you understand a kiss? Later, when we were in his father's car, he forgot about me again. They dropped me off at the tenement as if nothing had happened.

This Diary contains all that I don't know and all that I do know. Perhaps someday there'll be answers to all the questions I have today.

Does everyone feel this same turmoil when they're kissed for the first time? What does Alan feel for me? Why does he defend me, use me, save me, and then leave me in danger again? What would López Durán say in his next book if he found out about all this?

Thursday, March 26, 1987

I've just come back from a meeting between Fidel and some young intellectuals. It was pretty amazing. Some people asked for musical instruments, others told him about injustices they endured in the provinces. It was as though we'd all come to an agreement to complain at the same time.

Abdel talked about semiotic concepts no one understood, and Cuenca almost hit a lowly politician who wanted to shut us up, tell us what to do, and stifle our work.

After two days of meetings, and right in the middle of a tiring debate, I found myself sitting between Silvio Rodríguez and Gonzalo Rubalcaba. I was anguishing over the sheer number of problems we faced without solutions when I noticed how Fidel walked among us. He came down from the stage and touched the shoulders of several of the artists.

Nothing can happen to us now. This year, Carlos Varela was violently expelled from the movie house at 23rd and 12th Streets simply because of what he writes and sings. A few months back, they trapped some poets in a building in Matanzas. They turned the power off right in the middle of their reading and beat them to a pulp. They say it was a response to the frankness of their work.

Even Carilda Oliver Labra, who is very well known and respected, was hit in the attempt to silence them.

Fidel walked very slowly, reflecting on our catharsis. I wasn't feeling despondent. I had no emotion after we'd each had our say. I don't even know what I feel yet.

Who will promise us that everything will change? What's next for us? An opening, a holocaust, or the complete dispersion of all those who were here today? I fell asleep on the bus on the way back to Havana. The bus stopped in different neighborhoods along the way, letting artists out on the streets. The city smells fishy at dawn on these cold days.

When I got home, my mother's friends hugged me. It's as though I'd come home from war. I'm sure the whole conversation was leaked. It was hot news yesterday, but after tonight I don't know what will happen with all we were told. There were too many witnesses and too many problems.

None of the people who were at my house waiting for me had been invited to the meeting. They're not trustworthy, but I am. My God, what madness. My mom wants me to tell them something about what I experienced at the Convention Palace, but I'm too tired. I just want to write down what happened, so I don't forget it. It'll be better to talk tomorrow.

I did make one thing clear: "I feel lost. I have a feeling that we'll never see eye to eye."

I know too much. I feel too much. Perhaps in a few years I'll find an answer for these foggy and confused days.

There were moments when I asked myself what I was doing there. I was picked to go by my class, and the school sent me reluctantly. I had to say something, to show up, but I stayed quiet. There was nothing to add after what happened.

I've been carrying all this around in my head. I pour it all into my Diary because I need relief and because I need to postpone what I don't understand. That's why I always come back to these pages. Even if I want to stop writing, I come back. This is my favorite place, my refuge from war, my secret hideaway, my true confessor.

Friday, March 27, 1987

I came down from my room this morning. I sleep upstairs, on a cardboard loft. I have a map of stars hanging on one wall and on the other a tableau my mother made in 1970 of Alice in Wonderland.

All our friends are asleep on the ground floor. I try to make my way around them, but sleeping writers, painters, and producers block my way. There are people snoring everywhere. They cozy up, as always, on mats strewn around my mom's bed. Our little home looks like a battlefield. She calls this urban arrangement "Campismo leninismo": Leninist camping.

I don't feel like going to school. My head deserves a rest after everything that happened, but they're anxiously awaiting my return at school, too.

Our neighbor is very noisy in the morning. We rap the wall with the broom so she'll lower her voice. Every time her Russian lover comes to visit, she screams like a crazy person. I can't find the broom.

I don't know if I'll go back to the National School of Art as a residential student. I don't know what's worse: my house or the dorm. Everything is very dark because this apartment is deep in the tenement and gets very little light. I can barely see to write.

My mom is still asleep. It's a real chore to get her up early. I can't get into the bathroom. I have no privacy. I have no idea what it's like to be nude in my own room.

I go out to get a few buckets of water. This house is more inhospitable with each passing day.

I woke up my mother. I asked her to step outside so we could talk. There are too many people in here.

An Hour with My Mother

My mother is impossible. I try to explain things to her but there's no way. We went to the park on the corner, Martyrs Park, which is very open but private.

I asked if we could get rid of some of our visitors, to be alone together, without so many people occupying the little space we get to live in. I don't want to talk politics. I'm terrified of the political goings-on: after what I lived through last night, I'd rather keep a distance from all that.

My mother said that if I want to live without talking politics, I'll have to move to Canada, to a small village where it's very cold and people make a living cutting timber and aren't interested in knowing even the name of their country's president. According to her, Cuban politics are in what we eat, in what we wear, in where we live, in what we have, and even in what we don't have. For my mother, there's no possible way out: "If you want to escape politics, you have to escape from Cuba." She thinks that what we paint and write is political. She understands that I'm disoriented, but they can't keep getting on my case.

I don't know where my mother wants to go. I look at her and realize she can't live without her friends, without her routines at the radio station and the old people she tapes for "Words Against Oblivion" (which people always jokingly call "Words Into

Oblivion"). My mother rejects what she loves. I hadn't noticed that before. The revolution has always been her life, but since I've been able to reason, she's always been trying to leave. But to go where and why? I just want to stay away from politics. I can't stand to see myself in it. Something tells me I don't know how to fight at that level.

I walked back through the neighborhood, holding my mother by the arm. We took it easy because she's more easily distracted with each passing day. Cars go by and brush her dress and she's smug and in her own world. Where will I go if I ever want to get away from here? What will I do with my mother, who's already more like my daughter?

My mother talks about a neutral space, idyllic and nonexistent. She can quote Cummings by heart:

> somewhere i have never travelled,gladly beyond
> any experience,your eyes have their silence:
> in your most frail gesture are things which enclose me,
> or which i cannot touch because they are too near
>
> your slightest look easily will unclose me
> though i have closed myself as fingers,
> you open always petal by petal myself as Spring opens
> (touching skillfully,mysteriously)her first rose

or if your wish be to close me,i and

my life will shut very beautifully,suddenly,

as when the heart of this flower imagines

the snow carefully everywhere descending;

nothing which we are to perceive in this world equals

the power of your intense fragility:whose texture

compels me with the colour of its countries,

rendering death and forever with each breathing

(i do not know what it is about you that closes

and opens; only something in me understands

the voice of your eyes is deeper than all roses)

nobody,not even the rain,has such small hands

Saturday, March 28, 1987

Last night my mother and I were finally alone. No witnesses, no friends, no improvised chefs. We had to work really hard to transfer our usual guests elsewhere. They're almost all from the provinces and don't have a place to live in Havana, but we had to ask them for a breather. I need to walk around the apartment in my underwear and feel that I'm home, at least for a few days.

We made some pasta with garlic and soybean oil, toast, and instant Bulgarian soup. My mom opened a bottle of red Romanian wine that she calls "Ceaușescu's Revenge." I don't drink, but I tasted a little bit so we could toast to the two of us—so we can be alone together. She knows what that means.

My mom told me that the day I was born, the temperature was only seven degrees. It was the middle of winter in Havana. I was born between power outages and cold temperatures that December of 1970. When we left the hospital, there was nowhere to go. I didn't have maternal grandparents, and my father's parents in Cienfuegos couldn't take us in. Her best friend had a puppet theater in a nearby town, and that's where we ended up after a long ride that seemed to take us to the end of the world.

My mom says that by then there were no regular retail stores anymore, or things like hot chocolate, toys, layettes, and carnivals.

Everything was silence and stupor. The harvest of the impossible ten million tons of sugar was over; life had been postponed. The only thing that remained was a humid cold coming in from the sea and my mother dreaming of "the Europes" and the letters from friends who had left. That's why she decided to name me Nieve. I'll never forgive her for that. I've always felt ridiculous with this name. Every summer, as I swam at the beach, I'd hear my mother's shouts on the shore: "Nieve! Nieve! Nieve!" And when I got to the hot sand, I wanted to melt from embarrassment. With this heat, who would ever imagine giving a little Cuban girl such a name?

Only my mother.

I told her that the weirdest thing about my childhood was my closet. If I open it up and examine my old wardrobe, it can tell the story of my life and of my friends. One by one they've left me something to wear. Before leaving for Miami, Dania bequeathed me two pairs of blue jeans that I used well into adolescence, patching and fixing them along the way. Luckily, the most recent fashions didn't arrive here on time, and we could wear almost anything and get by. Now it's different, because we care more about what's in style out in the rest of the world. The news reaches us through the people who come and go. I remember the dresses from the sixties that my mom would carefully let out to create new and very strange variations. Fausto left several shirts that became coats for both of us.

My closet holds the traces of everyone who left and wanted to leave something for us.

The power went out. It's very early and my mother's asleep in the living room.

I know she misses her friends. I can't make her not have them over.

In many ways, my mother's still in art school, living amid the bunk beds and the student marches. It's best that I find my place somewhere else. This is her space, and I can't deny her the chance to create her world in this rough draft of a home—the chance to do it her way, as she's always done. I surrender.

Friday, April 3, 1987

Today I waited for Lucía outside a bar (the Angel of Tejadillo Street), and the building in front of it collapsed in an instant. It crumbled right in front of me. It just fell, all at once, leaving me there like a cracked piece of glass. Thrown on the ground, I could have been just one more dust particle blown away in Old Havana. I was thunderstruck. I felt so vulnerable. In fact, nothing really happened to me, but people carried me away to safety. They moved like a unified mass, all those people organized to "help." They put me in a green car, one of those antiques from the fifties, and sent me off to the naval hospital. Everything happened so fast, I didn't get a chance to think.

Lord God, it felt like Havana was falling apart, and then I remembered that my own home has been declared uninhabitable. What will happen to my mother and me? Perhaps we'll end up living in a shelter.

The doctors came to take care of me, but there was nothing wrong with me. Absolutely nothing. I was fine lying there on the stretcher, though I was scared. They asked for a phone number to notify my family, and that's when I realized I didn't have one and that my mother would never even know where the naval hospital is. She doesn't know the city well. She's easily distracted and she'll never find this place; she'll get lost. Finally, I got up and walked to Casablanca. I crossed the bay. I walked several kilometers just thinking about all this.

I knew, I definitely knew then that I couldn't let anything happen to me on the streets, because no one would come find me. I'm strong because I have no one.

When I got home, I was still brushing the dust off my shirt. I wanted to wash but there was no water. I wanted to call Lucía but there was no way.

Right now I'm sitting on a bench in front of the Habana Gallery, trying to write so I can calm down a little. I try to forget about everything like an amnesiac. I had to leave the gallery show because it contrasted too intensely with what had just happened. Inside that lit space, my friends are waiting for me: artists, people who clink their glasses, laugh, play, talk about things that I no longer have the energy to discuss. And in the meantime, back in the hospital, people I'm already forgetting are dying.

Lucía told me that she never reached the bar because of the building collapse. I felt shivers all over my body, and I asked her if I could borrow the expensive purple velvet jacket her grandmother had sent her from Madrid. Lucía took it off and put it around me (she is so special). And for the first time, I felt the velvet around me like a premonition. Now I'm a pauper transformed into a prince, but sometimes I'm a prince turned into a pauper. It seems my clothes have been deliberately worn out, that my boots have traveled an interesting and rough world. Would anyone who saw me believe that I, like Lucía (a good girl), had renounced all signs of luxury, of elegance, of order, even turned away the occasional glass of cider passed among the guests? I like this show of Japanese engravings. They're beautiful, erotic, ancient. But no one looks at the work during an opening. They only come to socialize.

I ran away. I'm in the park, writing. I'm sitting on a bench waiting for a bus or a ride to take me home. I'm not in the mood for intellectual jokes. I can see the gallery from here. People go in to look at everything except the work itself.

And there he is.

It's the third time I've seen him at the exhibition. Finally. He came on his motorcycle, making a violent noise, with his leather jacket flapping like the wings of an angel disguised as a demon.

Saturday, April 4, 1987

I saw him yesterday and I had to stop writing.

His loose hair frames his splendid Black-Asian face. The gallery's glass door didn't open. He simply went through it, intrepid, elegant, unreal.

I could be inside at the opening, toasting like everyone else, but no. I always run away. I have that strange habit.

I'm never in the right place at the right time.

Nieve in the Mirror

My eyes are long like almonds; I'm as light as a Japanese drawing.

My straight hair has grown, and now falls freely to my very small breasts, which contrast with my legs, my butt, my hips, and my very strong feet.

I'm a girl, a woman, but also a demon who recites incomprehensible verses and paints very badly. My room is a refuge, filled with toys and canvases. An adult life drowning in children's games. Who will I be? A little of everything, a little of nothing, a puzzle of lived experiences. I'm Nieve, snow in Havana.

Wednesday, April 8, 1987

It's six forty-five in the morning.

At dawn, the radio is a litany of complaints about everything in the world. Everything's wrong everywhere except in Havana. Fragrant tea waits for me at the table. I'm never going to forget the taste of brown sugar and bread. Or the canned fish chunks, or the flavorless flour, or the hard egg with white rice.

My mother continues to discover old boleros and anonymous sones. Each day she stops me as I'm going out the door so I'll hear the perfect and clean beat of the Septeto Habanero. They sing "Fuerza de voluntad le pido a Dios" like no one else. They leave you with a clear sense that time doesn't exist. It's true that those old guys never, ever, sing off key.

My mother folds in on herself in this dark place, surrounded by marginal people: ex-prisoners, whores, hustlers, workers, old retirees who get up at this hour to stand in an interminable line for a newspaper they never read.

But in this apartment with just one window and one door and only an interior view, marvelous things can still happen. The programs she writes here deal with Cuban music (the purest and most forgotten), mummies discovered in Egyptian catacombs, unidentified flying objects, and ghost ships on unknown seas. All of this is for the old RCA Victor microphones and Orwo tapes that come from Hungary, badly recorded for those listeners who get up at dawn eager for what's on the modulated frequency. A little later it'll all be forgotten. The marvelous things we cook up here always vanish in the wind.

Friends show up at the window, as do peeping toms who take pleasure in watching us sleep fully dressed. And through the door come only visitors: on layovers, from the provinces into the world, from the street to the station, from the bakery to the tenement, from the tenement inside the apartment, where we tell secrets.

In contrast with the darkness of my house, as soon as I open the door I'm blinded by the morning light. It's strange. My mother lives in the dark but people come to our home to ask her to shed light on things.

Saturday, April 11, 1987

It's been raining all morning. Very few professors came today and the school is flooded. I don't even know how I got here. I'm soaked.

I'm hanging out, painting in the red brick hallway, watching the rain fall.

Someone's here, kicking ass and taking names: Osvaldo. His motorcycle in the rain and his hair as black as his leather jacket and pants. The school improvised a welcome. My friends ran from engraving class to the sculpture studio while the women professors guided him under the cupola that looks like a giant architectural worm. That's the visual arts area. He speaks in a soft voice, his smile radiant.

The principal walked at his side while we all looked on, remembering his enormous paintings, his installations with many mirrors, his dead Che surrounded by wolves. The group approached me. Their laughter bounced off the circular cupolas. I wanted to run away to the golf course and leave all this stupid protocol behind, to flee and let the water drench me down to the bone, but he came up to me, his wet spiky boots marking their territory. He pointed me out with his finger. Everyone surrounded him. They seemed like a herd of horses, a swirl of ants checking out my easel. My God! And what I'm working on is awful—it's a truly lamentable watercolor. I didn't know whether to blot it out or die of shame.

I gasped when he complimented it, even though it's so insipid and impersonal.

Smells

I can still remember Osvaldo's smell: a blend of wet leather, oil paint, turpentine, and English lavender. I could feel his hair was wet. He offered me his hand and I trembled. There were traces of silver paint on his fingernails.

Now I'm home, swallowing my stinky boiled dinner and sitting in the rotten stench that comes from our neighbors. The power goes out again and the kerosene emits a black smoke that covers my body. It sticks to my hair. It follows me everywhere. The sound of my mother's typewriter lulls me to sleep.

She writes practically in the dark. I hope he didn't pick up this smell: kerosene, mildew, and violet water that my mother has bought ever since I was a child.

Havana smells of liquid gas and fresh fish from the salty air on the Malecón.

Sunday, April 12, 1987

My work is mediocre and everyone here knows it, but the professors are stunned by what Osvaldo said about it yesterday.

None of it makes any sense. Someday I'll quit painting, but I like school and I feel I should be here. It's the place for me right now.

Osvaldo has disappeared and so I walk around the grounds, ink-stained and alone. It rained all night, but I'm enjoying the dampness. I roll around on the red earth, my shirt open to let the sun into that unjust, inexplicable, and painful parabolic space that is the unintelligible trajectory of an unequal relationship. Osvaldo, Osvaldo, Osvaldo.

I fell asleep. I fell asleep wrapped in fear about what could happen. I dreamed that I gave my virginity away, that I gave it to Osvaldo in exchange for some tubes of black acrylic and three Canson cardboard sheets. It was a very casual exchange and my virginity was tucked inside a slippery see-through bag. I held it in my hands, showing it to Osvaldo, who wasn't giving me what he had promised.

I have to go home. It's late. It's getting dark.

Monday, April 13, 1987

(Everything that happened last night.)

I fell asleep on the grass yesterday. When I woke up, it was getting dark. I couldn't see the Visual Arts area. I could hear the showers and radios playing in the dorms. I went out to the road by the beach and waited an eternity for a bus. No one and nothing waited for me. I walked for hours along Fifth Avenue and finally cut through the dark streets of Miramar to shorten my journey. There was a particular music coming from one of the mansions. It was classic jazz, with good syncopation. I could hear plates clicking together and shrill laughter over the piano. I realized immediately that it was Frank Emilio playing.

The military guards at the house were on alert. The caravan of illustrious cars snaked over the raggedy lawn. I wanted to see what was going on inside. I climbed a nearby wall, then jumped over the fence. It was an ambassador's house, and they spoke Spanish. They seemed very courteous, light, natural, and refined.

They drank from tall, sculptured, colorful glasses, then cast them aside right in the open without finishing.

Suddenly, I realized I could blend in. I was so hungry and thirsty. There were so many people, I figured no one would suspect me.

But I also grasped, with great disappointment, that because I was wearing my school uniform it would be impossible to get past the guards. And attire aside, I was filthy, with ink stains and charcoal all over me. I was wearing red tights and the coat that Lucía had let me borrow, my ochre skirt and the school's white shirt. I made my way toward the small pool in the back, covered with dead leaves and abandoned because of an absence of children in the ambassador's home.

I took everything off at once and stood there naked, looking at myself in that silent mirror, calmly, like Narcissus. I hesitated, then broke through the glassy water and dove down, down, down, washing off the visible world, school, my mother, our home, our poverty, and my life.

I stayed for an hour in the clean depths, breathing like a naked fish, and leaving everything there—everything that wasn't useful for what was ahead—because something keeps telling me that everything's about to change for me. I shook my hair out in the chlorine's limp humidity and left part of my life behind as if I'd just crossed a border. I don't know what awaits me, but I don't care. Whatever will be, will be.

I pulled myself out of the water, dried myself with my uniform, then folded it and put it in my bag. I shook my head and let my damp hair loose like the women I saw in the distance coming and going with drinks in their hands. I left my ridiculous black bra behind; it was a gift from my mom, recycled from the sixties. I put on my red tights and fastened the bottom two buttons on the velvet jacket. I tied the laces on my black school-issue shoes, which just happen to be very trendy right now according to the fashion magazines (which I've seen at school), and that's how I entered the party. I became one more guest: very well put together, very fresh, and new. My intuition led me to think Moschino or Galliano. I was impeccable, Parisian. At least that's how I felt.

I immediately found myself before a sculptured form I was later told was caviar, salmon, and seven-grain bread. I choose a cup of cider and fig ice cream. Indescribable flavors: something smooth, spicy, sweet, savory, I don't know.

I danced with several men and talked about a thousand things with complete strangers. And then Osvaldo appeared out of nowhere. I must have been waiting for him. Finally, I was at the right place at the right time. This time he caught me stealing a piece of black candy from a dish on a baccarat table. He slapped my hand and licked the last drop of chlorine sliding recklessly down my recently washed neck. We talked, we danced, and at the end of the night, I left the embassy with him via the front door. The guard looked suspiciously at my red tights. He didn't recognize them. I stuck my tongue out at him and we left, totally drunk.

The motorcycle galloped down the avenue like a wild horse, and a deserted Havana seemed destined exclusively for us. We arrived in a strange neighborhood and dismounted in silence.

Suddenly, I realized I was trapped somewhere in another world.

Osvaldo's House

The house is huge, typical of the fifties, with bars and panels and glass bricks. Formidable couches adorn the rooms. There are servants' quarters and two guest bathrooms, an interminable labyrinth that I don't understand very well. The sculptures that I saw a thousand times in the gallery are here now, floating between glass panels in the corners.

When I saw myself in the mirrors, I looked frightened. I didn't look like me. Osvaldo played Talking Heads; I'd never heard of them before. Then Sting, singing in Spanish, and other new groups I've never heard anyone talk about. My musical culture is retro and stretches back to the most traditional Cuban styles.

Suddenly I smelled oil paint in the studio and had a flash of self-recognition. I was like a dog, sniffing out the trail until I found it. And then I found a nave filled with women. One resembled my body. In the drawing, she hid her gaze behind black glasses. She was fresh, like me. Soon that piece will be up for sale for who knows how much money.

The tubes of color were open, bunched up, forgotten. What luxury to have so much material that supplies can be left to waste like that. Ink sat next to brand-name brushes, soft and new. I couldn't believe it. I was overwhelmed by the turpentine (it always happens to me). I left the studio on the verge of depression. So much space, such perfect conditions for painting. My mother would say that working like that, anybody can paint a decent picture.

Osvaldo brought me an amber liquid on the rocks, but I asked him for a glass of milk instead. His smile made me blush. He quickly returned with a long white glass filled to the brim. I savored the pure and creamy milk. It had been years since I'd had anything like it. I don't want to compare his life with mine; it would be terrible.

Osvaldo's Room

The room is black. Both the walls and the floor, the sheets, and the stereo equipment. Black-and-white paintings surround the bed. There isn't a single photograph in the entire house. Osvaldo has no past.

The painter couldn't stop talking about himself the entire time. He talked about his work, his travels, his returns to the island; he always returns to the same point, to another island, to his island. And this one isn't remotely like the island in which I get up every

morning without breakfast and go to school on the other side of
the city. He was talking about another Cuba, another Havana,
another Nieve, the one he made up when he saw me—though he
never admitted it—in front of the gallery the day that building collapsed. He searched for me like someone looking for a blank sheet
on which to sketch.

Desire and Pain

Osvaldo kissed me very slowly as he talked about Paris. My black
eyes looked up at him without comfort. He smelled my clothes and
hair, he sought gold and diamonds between my legs. He was very
focused as he rooted in my red tights, and I opened up as if someone digging between my thighs was an everyday event. Confused,
he couldn't find his way in. I was sealed, though it seemed impossible, and my mundane movements suggested otherwise.

Osvaldo touched my small round breasts. A glass bead fell
from his neck and into my mouth, choking me. I swallowed with
terrible difficulty and chewed the rest without realizing I was bleeding. My tongue was purple and swollen. He thought of desire, and
I thought of pain.

I came out of my daze and bit his fingers. I wanted to swallow
all of him. I licked his arms and kissed his back. Black clothes fell

on the black floor. Osvaldo ripped my tights off me in anger and
my school shoes hit something somewhere that broke.

Then he trapped me on the floor. Cornered by his body, that's
how I felt. He was an old wolf ambushing a lost little hare. He bit
my breasts until I hit a delicious extreme of pain and pleasure. He
reached for the glass of milk that I'd left on the floor and poured the
rest over my pubis, which was drowning in desire, fear, and its own
virginity. His head went down so low I couldn't see it, and there
he awoke the most sophisticated sensations I'd ever felt: spasms
fragmented into a delightful pang. I swam in strange waters, an
involuntary panting turned into uncontrollable trembling. My legs
rose like flags, waved openly, freely, contrary to the secret puzzle
that resisted Osvaldo's entry. He was perplexed, but I didn't explain
anything. He'd find a way in.

Osvaldo came up on my chest emanating unknown perfumes,
aromatic oils, red concoctions that smelled of me. Frightened, he
asked me a question that I answered with a long, deep kiss. His
finger lit sparks in my bellybutton, my belly, and my feet. He took
me in his arms like a small child being taken from one bed to the
other in the wee hours of a feverish night. He lay me down in a tub
with hot and cold currents. The water pricked me like a thousand
needles. The trembling ceased with the steam and his hands rubbed

me wildly with strange pauses for kisses and tears that he tried to hide.

The painter wrapped me in a black towel, which smelled of lilies and naphthalene. He threw me on the bed, my hair dripping rose water, pure and fragrant, corrupted by my own uncontrollable and inevitable bodily fluids.

"No one's been here," he said, terrified, breaking the silence, trying to sink his tongue, then his index finger, in my sex. But I'm impossible to pierce, for now.

Osvaldo took a breath and launched himself like a warrior. He was aroused. I found him so beautiful that he could even have been loved by men; his splendor and courage would have provoked a runaway desire in any creature.

I was a minuscule pearl drowning in his oyster, trapped by lust and pain.

Pain has many degrees. A certain pressure made my sex convulse, open, and extend with a ravishing violence. I wanted to suffer that pain. I went mad as his sex made its way against the graceful resistance of my tiny but firm innermost shield. My anguish transformed into abandon while Osvaldo whimpered and caressed my hair with a tenderness rooted in the most delightful foolishness.

I bit his shoulder while my hands held on to the sheets, so that I wouldn't fall into the abyss I was already anticipating. Then, with an intuitive and lissome movement of my hips, a tenuous signal to continue provoked by a simple kiss on the forehead, he howled, breaking through my limits. A miraculous blizzard erupted inside me, taking me to a dimension where a path opens up that's very much like my words, my dreams, my breasts, and my knees; my movements and my birth.

Now I was like a deer born in the open fields, covered in blood and resin, transformed by a baptism of fire from virgin to goddess. Osvaldo exploded, holding me tightly to him so that I wouldn't flee; maybe he thought I'd fly away, leaving him alone with his white moon, a moon that rained inside of me.

We lay there, both of us complicit in this passion that lingers in my mind and which I write, write, write down so that I'll never ever forget.

I want to have it with me always, a gift I will pass down to all the women born in my family.

He sleeps while I write.

He's fast asleep as I barely begin the war.

Desire is pain abandoned in lust.

Friday, April 17, 1987

That first night, I never went back home; I don't think my mother missed me. I haven't been back in four days.

Now I'll never go back.

Today I'll go pick up my things. I don't know if I'm missed. My mother has so many friends to shelter, so many people to deal with in our home-refuge, that she may not even notice my absence.

I'll introduce my mother to Osvaldo.

Tonight, Osvaldo is having a dinner to introduce me to his friends.

A few have just come back from France. It'll be a marvelous night and, he tells me, I'll come to know his real world.

Saturday, April 18, 1987

My mother doesn't like Osvaldo. She disagreed with everything he said. She asked me why I had to leave home.

She thinks our place is a home and that our existence in it is a real life.

My mother begged me not to leave. She pulled me aside and told me not to trust Osvaldo. She has reasons not to trust men, but I don't.

My mom cried in the bathroom and I left with my hands practically empty. I suddenly realized I have nothing to wear to this dinner tonight. My God!

The Possibility of Choice

We arrived at Martyrs Park.

I felt bad leaving like that, as if everything that has been my life since we arrived from Cienfuegos meant nothing. My mother, our friends, the life I've led.

I asked Osvaldo to stop. I cried on his shoulder, but I couldn't explain why. I told him that none of the few clothes I'd gathered to bring with me would be good enough to be with him, much less to go to the dinner at his house tonight.

Osvaldo asked me to show him the clothes I'd brought from home. We opened the tiny red vinyl suitcase right there in the park. He looked at me and grinned, then he threw the whole thing into a nearby trash can, including my other school uniform. We left, flying on the motorcycle toward an unknown destination.

It's a weird feeling to cry while riding a motorcycle. Tears spill out all over the city; your face is like cellophane, twisted by the wind, and your life is in constant danger, all of which you're grateful for.

We went into a store for diplomats. I breathed deeply and discovered the source of the smell of Fausto's apples and curry. We ran to the clothing department. Osvaldo went looking, piece by piece, for things to create a new wardrobe for the new Nieve.

A black sweater.

Two pairs of black jeans.

Black boots.

Black underwear.

A black denim jacket.

Several black T-shirts.

A black dress for winter that is very elegant.

I'd never imagined that any of these things could be found in Cuba. In fact, today is the first time I've ever bought anything off the rack, the first time I don't have to tailor things. It's the first time that I've tried something on in a store to see if it fits. I didn't even know such a place existed.

Today Osvaldo showed me how to choose; how to choose whatever makes me different from the rest, from the masses, whatever makes me unique in the world.

Sunday, April 19, 1987

I'm back in school again.

Alan showed up in class and caused quite a scandal in front of everyone. Arte Calle rejects the art market, but Osvaldo sells all the time all over the world. What do I have to do with that?

I'm supposedly expelled from a group I never belonged to. Alan came to tell me I've betrayed my principles. Alan and my mother have always agreed on things, but for different reasons.

Now I wonder why my mom and Alan weren't mother and son. I've wished for a father like Alan Gutiérrez's every day of my life. That's how it goes. Everyone found out about my life with Osvaldo because of this scandal.

I'm in the dining hall, trying to write and eat this gruel. As I write, Arte Calle is outside, by the door, dressed in green and blue and pretending to march for Militiaman Day. Some people think it's in remembrance of Bay of Pigs, but those of us in the visual arts know it's just a performance.

I don't understand them anymore. Why do they do it? I continue writing; they don't matter anymore.

Osvaldo was quite embarrassed by me last night. There's no god on earth who can learn to eat with so much silverware. I talked

WENDY GUERRA   191

when I shouldn't have talked. I think he'd prefer I stay quiet, taking it all in until I can figure out how things are.

But that's not me. If that's how things are, then I'm in for a bad time. Disqualified.

Osvaldo's Friends

Jesús: Art collector and dealer, diplomat and histrionic actor in a theater group with an audience of no more than twenty people—us.

Lula: Jesús's wife. She repeats everything he says and then translates it into French, even though she's Cuban and we understand her in Spanish.

Cleo: An excellent poet. She won't look at me. To her, I'm probably something along the lines of a flying cockroach. She quotes from the verses of great French poets. She wears huge hats. She's not ugly, but she's not pretty either. I can forget her face but I can't forget her.

Aurelia and Lía: A couple of feminist painters. Aurelia was married to Osvaldo for twelve years. When he left her, she met Lía, who was her student, and now they live together. They paint and give a lot of parties in a small studio in a corner of the house. There's no way to hide from them. They're always there, judging you. They're pedantic and cultured. I give up.

At the dinner, they asked me what neighborhood I was from. After I said Cayo Hueso—on Jovellar and Espada—they didn't look at me for the rest of the night. And to think there are no class differences in Cuba.

They talked all night about Osvaldo's trip to France. It seems he's leaving for a while. Since I don't exist, I don't talk. When I try to offer an opinion, Osvaldo opens his eyes wide in warning.

I'm very good at getting scolded. I think my mother might be right, that this world is quite superficial. I went to bed before they left.

Wednesday, May 20, 1987

I was awakened by Jesús today. It was barely eight in the morning. He came into our room; apparently, he has keys to the house. Osvaldo was out and I was nude, asleep on the bed. Jesús barely looked at me. He barely said good morning as he took the black-and-white paintings from the room. Bit by bit, he emptied the room while I was still in it. He even moved the bed to get at a drawing that was hanging behind me.

When Osvaldo came home and saw what was going on, he was furious with me.

Jesús is in charge of his sales and his professional life. How could I get in the way of his getting the paintings? Osvaldo scolds me but he doesn't say anything to Jesús. That would be inconvenient.

I went to visit my mother today. I went without Osvaldo. She can't stand him. I took her one of his first engravings, from the series he made when he graduated. Surprise: my mother looked at the piece and tore it to shreds. She just kept talking as she tore it, like there was nothing wrong.

There's no way out of the situation with my mom. She talks about a thousand things at once, loses her train of thought, then blurs the stories that she forgets along the way. She asked me to move back home. She thinks there's still time before I turn into a little monster.

She says all those diplomat friends of Osvaldo's are just living off communism, that they don't believe in squat, that they're not real Communists. She hates seeing me mixed up with these people, and she hates my being involved with art dealing even more. "Painting is something else, Nieve." My mother has always been so honest! I can't help but feel the weight of her words.

Our apartment on Jovellar smells very bad. I have trouble swallowing what my mom offers me to eat. Even the birthday cake. I feel guilty. What am I going to do with myself? I don't even understand myself anymore.

I'm reading while riding the #27 bus to Nuevo Vedado. My mother lent me a book by Nélida Piñon. My mom never lends something without a reason. What she's highlighted reminds me of the dinner party I told her about.

It's imperative to applaud the human talent
that adorns the silver trays with the best of their efforts.
In terms of the dinner itself, reality, approved of by
the restless guests, lubricated my feelings
and buried them in a stupor until the next day.

Thursday, May 21, 1987

I don't know what being in love is about. I get a feeling, then lose it.

Now it turns out that Osvaldo has banned my Diary, just like my father. He read everything I wrote about his friends, found out what my mother thinks of him, and became enraged. I don't want to argue; I hate to fight. Machismo in Cuba is veiled by our high level of education, but it's still there, threatening you all the time, between pretense and reality.

I don't understand why Osvaldo and my father hate the Diary. History repeats itself to remind me that I've never been a master of my own fate.

I barely have time to jot down what I'm going through. Everything happens so fast but haste doesn't preclude reflecting on events.

There's so much passion and excess in everything around me, and much of it is out of my control. I don't have time to write it all down because censorship comes with every man that crosses my path.

Razor in the wind
Someone
Always
Comes

And cuts
My favorite
Pants.

It's always him, the same man, with his razor in the wind
lacerating my body

the razor's edge, my own fear.

Alan's Farewell

It's raining like mad.

We've closed up the house. And then I heard hard knocks on the window of the front door. Osvaldo and I had spent the entire morning arguing because of the incident with his friends. I hate the idea of giving up my Diary, fighting, and repressing my way of doing things. I can't seem to figure out how to live as a couple. I have a hard time harmonizing, even when I want his company. He hasn't been able to tame me. It only took a bit for Osvaldo to fall asleep, exhausted by my crying and pleading.

I went to open the door and it was Alan. He'd come to say good-bye. I couldn't believe he'd dared to scale our wall. I also can't believe that I won't see him everywhere anymore, that he won't be within my reach. I've come to the realization that he always shows me what's really real, and that I chose to escape to this aseptic cupola where I try to hide, so I won't feel like I'm in danger.

The only person who ever honestly asks me to be happy is leaving. He's been showing me his wounds and I've been curing them with my tears since we were kids. He always thought I was fragile, not realizing that I saved all my vulnerabilities for him. Now it's too late.

He's going to Mexico, maybe en route to Miami. He broke up the group because, little by little, almost everyone is leaving.

He came to get me to go to the going-away party. I told him I would, but he knows it's a lie. I've never gone to those kinds of parties, and I'm not going to start by going to say good-bye.

Alan kissed me on the mouth. He pulled me away from the door and into the garden. The water was coming down so hard, I could barely see him. The only things I could make out were his anxious eyes, pleading for something I couldn't figure out. I slapped him for that abrupt kiss, which is so his style, but I hit him hard anyway. Then we both started to cry and hit each other.

Alan jumped over the wall again and left me alone, soaked in front of my new house. In that instant, I just wanted to die, but I had no choice but to make my way stealthily to the bathroom. I dried myself with a towel, and then I sat and wrote down everything that happened, stifling my sobs, putting everything down on paper.

Good-bye, Alan Gutiérrez

You're not tired of this ardent effort.

You, seductive fallen angel.

Don't evoke enchantments that will forsake me.

Winter 1988

Incident with Cleo

Cleo has come to eat with us. She's fallen asleep on the couch while Osvaldo and I wash the dishes. Of course, she's done it on purpose—she's capable of this and much more. You just have to read her to figure out what she's up to.

I woke her up and asked her to go sleep in the studio, on the small guest bed. She quickly took off her clothes, except for her black underwear. She walked around the house, asked us for water. She talked nonstop, saying crazy stuff, as if she was a somnambulist.

I've been warned about her. This poet has to be watched.

I put some Chinese silk sheets on the little bed. I want her to be cold and go home at dawn. I cranked the AC to the max, so that it's practically freezing. It's an old American AC, from the fifties, which is why that old gringo does such a better job blowing cold air than all those newer Russian machines.

When we went to bed, I asked Osvaldo for the first time ever not to leave the room, not even to pee; I was a little upset. At three fifteen in the morning, Cleo came into our room. She threw herself down between us and pulled up the blanket. She kissed each of us and went back to sleep like a little girl.

I don't understand a thing. I spent the night thinking. Osvaldo looked happy.

But I, in turn, felt trapped.

NOTE

It's six in the morning. Osvaldo and Cleo are asleep in the room, in the same bed under the same blanket.

I make coffee while I question my doubts. I don't really understand what's going on.

I get that my Diary is banned from this relationship, but these pages are the only place where I can vent. It's always been that way, even in the worst of times.

For the last four months, I've written very little. I don't want to date things; the whole week is one big adventure. This house is like a movie. I don't need to travel. I live in a pretend Europe in the middle of the Caribbean. If I want to feel a part of "the world," I need to stay in this circle and not feel so disappointed, much less lose heart.

Life out there contradicts my new status. It contradicts this fantasy. Life here denies my mother's life, and that of my classmates who have to survive living in the dorms at the National School of Art. Out there is another country that a girl like me can't ignore.

Now it's seven fifteen in the morning and I need to go to school. I let Osvaldo and Cleo sleep. They're adults; there's nothing else I can do. I can't behave like a stupid and incoherent peasant. They're trying to bait me, and I'm not going to fall for that.

I ask myself how many times I've slept in the same bed with my friends during exceptional situations. Of course, this is not an exceptional situation. Maybe they're just a different kind of people and this is the price I have to pay to be accepted.

I don't know what's wrong with me. I can't seem to find a place that fits me, that reflects who I want to be, how I want to feel.

I'm on my way to school. There's no point in complaining now. I think maybe it's a little late to try and understand these adults.

Surprises

There were three surprises when I got home from school.

1) Cleo's poetry book has just come out in Spain and she left me a copy with a very personal dedication. I guess I passed her test.
2) The news that Osvaldo will be leaving for Paris for several months.
3) Jesús has asked that my papers be processed so I can go with Osvaldo. But I'm still a minor, and my father can't give his consent. Basically, I can't leave Cuba until next year. There's

no way to escape. Everything's been the same since 1980. Even though the years go by, we're beached on the same shore.

Hanging around the Galleries

I went to Flavio's show with Cleo. Flavio is an exceptional painter from an extraordinary generation. I met him in Cienfuegos when I was little. I also met Bedia and Tomás. I always knew we'd meet again, but he doesn't remember me. He's a professor at school, where he's much admired and followed. No one misses his shows because he's a great maestro. He launches his concepts and wisdom out like a lure, and here we are, trapped in his net. Flavio is the axis of a generation that changed art, thinking about art, and even how to be an artist in Cuba. Though we see each other at school, he doesn't recognize me, and maybe that's my fault. I've changed so much. I'm just not the same.

With Osvaldo gone from Cuba, I feel weird going to galleries alone, but I also feel a certain freedom.

These have been strange days: they've closed many shows. The police don't let people exhibit even in their own homes. My mother called to warn me not to exhibit political work. She wants peace of mind. I haven't painted in a long time, about two years, but she doesn't know that. Things are ugly. I always get the feeling that something awful could happen when I go see a gallery show. I always run into people from school and I have a good time, but the situation is tense.

Cleo gave me her opinion of the show we saw today, and I gave her mine without too much protocol. It was more my opinion about what's been going on with the galleries since last year. And with the painters on G Street. It's pretty clear that neither the intellectuals nor the writers are in the vanguard of contemporary Cuban ideas. The visual artists are the vanguard. They push and force open society's doors, no matter how tightly shut they are.

Cleo thinks I should write about my ideas; she thinks perhaps I could be an art critic. She admitted that when she spent the night at the house, she peeked in my Diary. I was paralyzed with shame, but she says I write very well. My mother says the same thing, but I don't believe her. It's very childlike to believe your own mother's praise. The applause is much too close-up.

Cleo invites me out to eat every night. We're both alone in the city. She's been reading me her novel a little at a time. At the end of each night, she reads me a new poem, which is my favorite part.

I always dress in black and walk by myself through the deserted city to hear Cleo.

Good-bye to Cleo

The night that Cleo finished reading me the end of her story, I realized that she'd been planning her escape. It's impossible to tell so many truths and continue to live in Cuba. She is unpublishable here.

When she described her protagonist in the nude, with a mole in the form of a butterfly between his legs, I knew she was picturing Osvaldo. It's clear that her Manuel is my Osvaldo. I have no doubt now that they were lovers at some point. Perhaps they still are, who knows.

My mother is right about many things: this world is not right for me. I'm tired of trying to explain my boyfriend's friends' morals, ideologies, and aesthetics ad infinitum.

The poem that Cleo read to me was perfect. It was just as I was going home, the same night that I heard the end of her novel. Cleo is a great poet, I can't deny that; I'm incredibly moved when she reads. It's as though everything she reads to me recalls another time. Her words are confident, intense, delicate. The piece was about how we destroy a poem the minute we begin to write it, how we kill it with our very own hands the very instant we try to imagine it. I admire Cleo so much. When she writes poetry, she's the best.

Walking Back to Nuevo Vedado

Cleo has given me six hats I carry in a single bag; I must buy the seventh in Paris on a Sunday afternoon. I believe this is a farewell. Perhaps I can tell precisely because of the routine of saying good-bye in which I've been raised. I gave her a poem I wrote dedicated to her. My first serious text, my leap into the abyss. I left it with her in a sealed envelope so that she'll read it in Paris. We kissed good-bye in silence, without a word about it. She, too, is afraid of microphones. I'm walking home. I think about everything that I'm losing, so that I can perhaps regain it later. But who knows.

Even Osvaldo is blurry to me now: it's been nine long months since I've seen him. I've almost forgotten his face. When he calls me on Saturdays, he tells me all about the friends who keep arriving in Paris; there's hardly anyone left here anymore. Aurelia and Lía are in Mexico. Jesús is still in Paris. There really aren't many artists left here. They've been fleeing since the witch hunts around the exhibitions.

I hope Osvaldo can get me out of here soon. My feelings only last a certain amount of time; if they're not cultivated, they'll disappear. I don't trust anyone. I don't wait for anyone. That's how I was raised, and that's how I am.

Things have never gone the way my mother and I plan them.

During my childhood, I said good-bye to all my friends. Today I said good-bye to Cleo. As I was trying on her most beautiful hats, one after the other, I knew her departure was definitive.

How many more friends must I say good-bye to before I can make my own escape? As a sign of respect, I took off her hat.

Have a good trip, my dear Cleo.

Winter 1988

I'm still going to galleries.

Someone stepped on an image of Che at a show I went to tonight.

Someone was taken to prison for stepping on an image of Che on the floor of an art gallery. They said it was one of the guys from Arte Calle, but I'm not sure.

I walk briskly over La Rampa every single day, stepping on the tiles on the ground. Every day thousands of people step on the work of Wifredo Lam and Luis Martínez Pedro, but it's not the same. They lie. Art and politics are very different. No one can step on the image of a hero. I don't know if it was a performance. The work was there and, in the confusion, someone felt enough ownership over what we had always been told was our patrimony that they thought it was fine to step on it, but that gesture was seen as humiliating. But if the image was on the floor and someone just casually walked over the very foundation of everything that has happened, it could be seen as something beautiful, something normal. If it had been a catharsis, I would have understood it that way. Che is every day, every day in every home in this country. His asthma and his madness, his suicidal soul. Everything he said and all he broke through because of his irreverence don't compare in the slightest way with stepping on his image. How many things did he transgress? Somebody put his foot on the image of "The Heroic Guerrilla," walked firmly over everything that had been prohibited, and the world ended over here. The gallery is closed. Of course, it's become fashionable to close galleries. What a pity.

Today I'm going to look through the glass, put my nose right up to it, and see if Che is still on the floor, stepped on or victorious. I just want to know if they've left him there, on the floor.

My Graduation

I graduate Friday and also get evaluated to pass to the next level. That would be the Institute of Art, but I've been burning bridges and no one imagines I'll still be in Cuba when the first year starts.

I've prepared a piece inspired by the work of a friend, Juan Carlos García. Now I just have to figure out how to order the library. I've built enormous bookshelves. I've covered some, not others. The shelves look like giants who'll be burned on the day of graduation on the school's campus. I've covered about a thousand books and the rest are out in the open. Marxism, science fiction, esotericism, history, mathematics, political science, scientific communism, romance novels, contemporary novels, Kant, Aristotle, and several other philosophers and thinkers.

My mother says she doesn't want to know what will happen to that mass of paper. It pains her to watch books burn. She told me it reminds her of the Cultural Revolution in China. She doesn't support my thesis, even if it opens the way to reflection.

But in the end, it's my work, and it's ready. All that's left is to light it and ask the saints to not let it rain.

The Waiting Period

My mother calls every morning to tell me which Eastern European government has fallen today. She's enjoying it like a great show.

Osvaldo doesn't call from Paris so often anymore. But when he does, he asks me to prepare to travel. I take care of delivering messages to the spouses of the other painters; they're getting out little by little. I don't want to implicate anybody in my Diary. I also don't want to discuss my plans in detail.

You have to be very quiet and very discreet to get out of Cuba these days.

It's us, the artists, who are in the spotlight right now. There are more informants than critics among us. I hardly ever leave the house anymore. I don't visit anyone because the vast majority of my friends have left. Lucía and her mother are now in Madrid. They left without a word. There are going to be very few of us from our first-year class who'll actually graduate from school.

Jesús continues to sell Osvaldo's work and get grants to prolong the stays abroad of all the artists who left with him. He managed to get the Mitterand Foundation to support them. His project is going forward.

Cleo's book is about to come out in France.

The only thing left for me to do is say good-bye.

My phone book is full of red ink. I can't dial those numbers anymore. Nobody would answer. I hardly know anyone left in the city. Everyone's leaving. They're leaving me by myself. The telephone doesn't ring anymore.

I'm waiting my turn, quietly.

Burning Bridges

I received the highest possible grade. Everything turned out exactly as I thought it would and how my advisers imagined it. The fire next to the school's cupola looked magnificent.

But, in fact, they didn't approve me for admission to the Institute of Art. I understand. My work these last few years has been mediocre. This final project doesn't make up for all I didn't do in the past.

"I feel a great lack of interest in everything that's going on here."

As the books burned, I realized that my bridges were burning too, one at a time. I thought about all the writers throughout history whose work has been incinerated. A book by Marx was in flames next to one by Milan Kundera. What madness. I think my project was well-liked because it was a big idea. I feel it was worthwhile.

The professors were respectful and even proud of my piece. I wanted to say thank you before I shut the door behind me. Here I've learned to order the very thoughts that went up in flames, perhaps to start from nothing and create something that's truly mine. This is a way of saying all that's caught in our throats.

When Osvaldo called on Saturday, he didn't ask about my graduation. He's forgetting me little by little. I get cooler every day and ask myself where I'm going and with whom.

There were only five graduates from our freshman class of twenty. We were all very solemn, quiet, practically taking a moment of silence for those who had left.

I came back home, alone and somber. One day after the other, waiting to see what will happen.

Good-bye to My Mother

As I go into my house, I run into Mauricio right at the door. He's leaving; he has a grant to study languages in the principality of Malta. We wish him good luck. My mother is very sad; she's losing her best reporter. We know he won't be coming back.

But my mother knows me very well and guesses that my hour has come and that I'm leaving, too. I'll fade slowly from her photographs, as she always says happens to those who leave her life forever and enter the world.

I turned eighteen yesterday and I'm now waiting for my "freedom pass." My mom doesn't want me to get it because she doesn't like Osvaldo. It'd be impossible for the three of us to ever live together—they both push my emotions to extremes.

We stare at each other's faces. We're experts in saying goodbye, but it's not the same when it's between the two of us. I never imagined this moment would come.

The papers will be ready in a month and then Osvaldo will come get me.

Everything has come to an end.

The end of school, the end of my house in the suburbs, the end of speaking in codes.

My mother told me not to come say good-bye before leaving, that she'd rather not see me again after today. "My arms are tired of farewells," she said. She didn't hug me. She climbed up on my loft and asked me to leave the door ajar, in case anyone else wants to come in and say good-bye.

I cried all the way to the Malecón. I remember the day I was taken to the orphanage, that other day she wouldn't say good-bye. I'm not sure what I feel. I'm so lost, and I don't know what to do with everything I've been storing inside me. But one thing is clear.

There's nothing else for me in Cuba. I'm leaving for my own good, for Cuba's own good. I feel such strange things, as if it's the end of my country.

Since I've been able to reason, my mother's been training me to leave and forget.

It's time.

Winter 1989

Why bother to write in my Diary. So many months on strike with nothing to say. Six months to get permission to leave the country, six more and Osvaldo still hasn't found a way to come and take me with him. I don't know who to believe anymore. The mail is slow. I don't want to include the letters in this Diary—it would be too painful to see how we've lost steam over time, how his lies become obvious, how he edits what he tells me...As time passes, there are fewer calls, and I feel his voice less and less with my body, and desire escapes with one pretext after another.

I'm still the keeper of his memory. But I'm becoming more and more silent. I don't write, I don't paint, and I don't open up the house unless I absolutely have to.

I spend more time with my mother; now I'm back where I used to live. I'm terrified of what might happen to me. I don't trust Osvaldo or his friends. The airport is the Bermuda Triangle and Paris is a metaphor; it doesn't exist. Where have they taken all my friends? I knock on doors that no one answers. And I keep crossing out numbers in my little red phone book.

At least I can come back here and jot down what's happening, if anything actually happens.

I've said good-bye so many times and nothing happens, except that I continue to be anchored here.

Winter 1989

At my house in Cienfuegos and the apartment on Jovellar we've always listened very quietly to Spain's Radio Exterior and the Voice of America. My mother never used to let me know anything because I was very indiscreet as a girl and would just yak away at school. Now that time has passed, she doesn't censor things. Spain's Radio Exterior has announced the fall of the Berlin Wall. The barriers come crashing down, people beat them down with whatever they have on hand, and the whispered commentary comes at us like an epidemic; people bring news as they come and go from their house to school and from school to the streets. The newspapers here have very little to say about any of this. I'm not in the habit of reading them. My mother says that someday she'll crumble like the Berlin Wall, that she doesn't have the strength to put up any more partitions. She doesn't know how to live without separations, without barricades. She feels protected by walls even though she hates them; she lives behind the ramparts. If capitalism ever arrived on these shores, if the wall of water around us fell, we would have to learn another way to survive. My mother would not be able to deal with it. She has spent a lifetime complaining about being choked off from the world, but there's no doubt it's a love-hate situation to which she's become accustomed.

People here are mostly glad for the Germans who are reunited, for the entire families that get to return to their homes, but we also wonder what's going to happen to us. We're propped up by these very walls; where would we be without them? Where will all this end? The sound of the radio comes and goes. The voices from Berlin seem anxious. The Spanish announcer says that seventy-nine people have already lost their lives attempting to return.

There's no question my mother is afraid of the future. She's euphoric and confused. Our friends who studied in the Soviet Union always said the same thing: It's been over, for years. Now it's just bricks tumbling to the ground, family reunions, everyone going back. My mother's eyes are glassy. I can't imagine how we would break through the wall of water, amorphous and deep.

We have to wait for more news, but I don't know if more information will come.

She's tormented. What will happen to us? Her black eyes lock me in, question me; she's so confused. She can't help but light a cigarette and stare at the bookshelves. My mother always has the right text for everything and every minute in the universe. She got off the couch and grabbed a book that was falling apart. She sat back down and put her legs on mine, stretched them out, then read slowly, nervously.

If by chance I contradict myself

in this confused erring,

one who has been in love

will understand what I say.

—Sor Juana Inés de la Cruz

"A Rational Description of the Irrational Effects of Love"

January 10, 1990

I finally went to the house today.

There were several calls and much insistence from the Film
Institute. They said someone was doing a documentary on Osvaldo.
His friends were adamant, but I didn't answer until this morning. I
don't know why I agreed without first getting an okay from Paris; I
just did it, strictly of my own accord, because I had a presentiment.
I drank my coffee, answered the phone, and said, "I'll wait for you
today."

A man with a camera showed up. He's too beautiful for this
place. It's impossible for me to be closed up in this glass box with
him. I feel clumsy. I bump into things; I'm disgusting when I'm
this insecure. What was seduction like again? I've forgotten. I
unveil one painting after another. They're stuck together because
of the time that has passed. I unroll the canvases. The smell blinds
me. I can remember the precise details of each piece, even what we
ate at dawn when each work was completed. I look at him and feel
I should say something…about these things I'm showing a stranger
with a camera.

I realize it now: this living room is a glass box. The glass table
reflects me in the aquamarine hues from the fifties. Osvaldo and
I would eat here, sitting on the floor, our backs against the black

couch. We had a ritual of tossing things aside, then I would spread myself over this large table, opening my school uniform so that he could take me like a birthday gift, my legs like ribbons coming loose from his desire. I no longer think about desire; I don't touch myself.

No one will believe that I've been faithful to Osvaldo all this time. My Diary and I know it's true, although sometimes I come off like a naughty girl.

The man with the camera has light eyes. I noticed the minute he got here, though he only looks at me through the lens. He's so tall, I can't reach him. I'm just dust when he walks next to me, always looking through the viewfinder, capturing objects, light, shapes, colors, textures.

He walked through the whole house, filmed the catalogs. He didn't want anything to drink. He didn't even look at me for the first two hours. No one needs to tell me that if it's a documentary about Osvaldo, I'm just a shadow. And everything else is a blur. I had set myself up in the bedroom to quietly finish writing about last night when he came in looking for me and sat on the bed.

How does one film in a black room without enough light?

I went mute. I don't have permission to let anyone film in the bedroom, there are too many paintings in here. Jesús took about half of them, but I've been slowly substituting what's missing with our personal outlawed collection, erotic like the Pompeiian underground.

I'm busy thinking. The man aimed his camera and told me to keep writing. Notes and scribbles, that's what I wrote down, but that page will disappear the minute I finish with it.

Little by little, the voyeur took the room from me, stealing images. God, I'd left my underwear draped over the stereo cabinet and he even snooped there. I like this kind of shame.

When lunchtime rolled around, I set the napkins on the glass table. We settled there. I hadn't even asked if he was hungry.

Scrambled eggs and ham. Raw chard with onions and soy sauce. Peaches in syrup pulled from a jar of Bulgarian preserves that taste like they've been stored in a can in a warehouse and mixed with some kind of hair product. It's hard not to notice. Linen napkins and tablecloth. Water in the amber glasses, and silence during the meal.

His name is Antonio. He filmed me as I ate because he couldn't help himself. He's drawn to one image after another. Content is something else. He'll figure out where it goes later, when he has the structure laid out: a place for everything.

When I put the coffee on the table, he spilled the sugar and used his fingers to draw me, even the square lines of my haircut. It was a drawing in six parts extended over the length of the glass, and perfect.

We talked about my Diary, about his childhood in an aris-
tocratic suburb, about his mother who wears her hair like mine
in black-and-white photos, about his desire to be a painter, the
Russian circus, and the day he met Popov the clown because he did
a poster for them. He talked to me about his most recent short and
we found we had friends in common. I thought that perhaps we
should have met somewhere, but then realized I would have already
left a few minutes before. Coming and going but not coinciding. I
told him I was in a long process of farewell and he said he's never,
ever, going to leave.

He finally asked me what I couldn't answer.

"What are your plans in Paris?"

I had absolutely no response for him. I could have said love, but
besides being an overly simple explanation, it wasn't true anymore.
Too many months, too much silence, too many experiences on his
part while I was at a disadvantage the whole time. I suddenly realized I was alive right now, that with Antonio I was in the real world.

I couldn't answer him, I couldn't answer myself. Two tears
slowly rolled down my face, confirming what I was feeling but
couldn't express. Paris had slowly stopped making sense, had van-
ished in a puff of air. Antonio slid up and kissed my two tears with
his fleshy lips. He kissed my face with great care. I trapped his lips
with mine and kept us from separating for a long time.

I thought that I was swallowing life in its entirety, that I was giving him my desire as a gift and that he was giving me his in return, his spit tasting of loquat and mint, of manliness, salt, poma apple. We drank each other up all at once; we were thirsty, sleepy.

It was so late, and we'd spent the whole day together. We could barely stand to separate. But I had nothing else to give him, nothing he could film so he'd stay with me. Everything we'd been in that glass box ended in a moment. It was over, that's what I thought.

"Please lend me your Diary," Antonio said, as if he were trying to understand something.

"No, no, no," I said, nervously.

And I let him go, terrified because I thought he wouldn't come back.

As soon as I closed the door, I went searching in the trunk under the stairs and randomly pulled out two notebooks, then grabbed the one that was lying on the bed. When I opened the door to run after him, he was still there, standing in the wet garden, waiting for me, waiting for the notebooks. It had been raining and we hadn't noticed.

I don't know, I don't know, I don't know how in the world I've given him this Diary. I have to be honest, at least here: I entrusted him with three volumes. I always hide my Diary from men, but today I gave them to a complete stranger, someone who came to film and said his name was Antonio. A loan, to lend my underwear, my life, my hideouts, my secrets. How could I do this?

I can't sleep.

The phone is ringing. Maybe it's Osvaldo. It's already morning in Paris.

January 11, 1990

Last night, I fell asleep after talking with Antonio. He called, he made the move. I was still, like a little girl wrapped in those black sheets. But shivering.

We talked through the night. He wants to respond to what he read in my Diary.

He thinks it's intense to have my life in a Diary, that it's as complete a work of art as Osvaldo's. He asks me why I'm still silent. What am I hiding from?

To do: He asked me to get a copy of *Jardín*. I haven't read *Jardín*. I remind him of Bárbara, enclosed behind the fence at her house. I know that house on Línea Street. I visited that junky garden with my mother. It has a small chapel to the side. They've walled in the chapel now, but it was open before; anyone could freely enter that little temple. That house used to be a symbol of a generation that left in another way. Cloistered in their marble, they left while staying here. Linen tablecloths and perfectly placed cups, as if nothing had happened. Outside, the people undid their longtime habits, but inside they continued with dinner at a predetermined hour, eating a dollop of rice with a full set of silverware, holding on to their memories and counting on patrimonies that had irredeemably fallen apart. A founding family, a dead garden. The last days, a house collapsing on itself without a chance of being propped up somehow. I want to read *Jardín*. I want to know what Bárbara's like.

I should be able to find an old edition of *Jardín* among the booksellers at the Plaza de Armas. Dulce Maria Loynaz still breathes in another walled-off house, the one on E Street. She's alive right now. I can't believe it: I walk by the wall and I can feel the noise coming from the crumbling house. In spite of everything, she's still there, impregnable and imperative, all the while refusing to leave her space. She's flown more missions ostracized and in the margins than many war pilots in the spotlight.

When I go out on the street, the light blinds me. I know that right now, Antonio is reading me while I look for him among the old books for sale.

NOTE

Did my mother and Antonio's mother ever know each other in the sixties?

January 13, 1990

A friend calls me and tells me to be careful with Antonio. He's problematic and has already been warned because of the content of his documentaries. Plus, he has one great defect: he's prettier than he is smart.

I explain that it was Jesús's office that sent him to make this documentary, which they need to debut in Paris; it's an interesting way of promoting art. In fact, they're going to have documentaries made of all the artists who went with Jesús on that project.

My friend warned me about being naive. She says Jesús plays for both teams, and that he's flirting with the fact that Antonio is seen as "complicated." She tells me I should learn to deal the cards or get out of the game.

Oh, Jesús, I'm so tired of your messages in the air, unfathomable to someone who isn't even twenty years old and has to figure out their inherent paradox. Where will you end up? How come they let you do and undo whatever you want? How will I ever understand a country that judges my mother so gravely but is so lenient with this sort of man?

I'm cautious with Jesús, but to be careful with Antonio would require being careful of what I want to be. I need to keep these things alive in my Diary. If I don't see him again, he can't appear in these pages again, and that would sadden me—it would annul me. His kisses leave me up in the clouds, and his ideas fill my lost pages. When I'm not writing, it's because his gaze is upon me and I'm amazed. I look at his work and read through a few rough drafts of stories he wants to film if he can get the funding.

A call from Paris; everything's the same. Very cold, few gigs. I wait; Osvaldo is alive. I read *Jardín*, wander, and take notes.

NOTE

I wonder what Antonio is like in the nude. When I touch his back, I feel like I travel to unknown dimensions. When I undress every day, by myself, I do it for him. I pose and walk like the woman he'd project in his personal movie.

January 20, 1990

Antonio finally ripped my red skirt. I can't say more than that, but I'm also dying to tell it, to tell it all. I'm afraid of the Diary and its consequences. I fear what I adore. I'm in a panic about being discovered, and I find myself lifting the veil.

The house is the moon leaking onto the mirror.

The parks aren't parks but living things. His films have become my obsession.

What about Paris? What's wrong with me?

Antonio undressed me in the middle of the living room and made love to me on the floor, leaving it damp with all we'd worked up together, desperate. He went straight to the spot where all my pleasures reside, where the women from my family tree live, disoriented and aroused. That's where I'm from, from that brutal pleasure that frees me; where my daughter will be born, and where I'll let her go, all the way to where I'm most myself, where my body turns into that greater pain which is me and which sublimates Antonio without remedy, without lies.

I take three deep breaths, just as he's asked me to do, whenever I burst into tears from pleasure, guilt, or forgiveness. He's brought back my Diaries, but he doesn't want to respond just yet. He's asked me to live, and that changes my shaky handwriting, my fear of everything.

Forgive me, Diary, if I don't write anymore. This is a time for living. I don't want to lie, but I also can't speak about what's going on. Everything is happening, that's the best I can do to describe things.

The sea is flooding the city and I won't try to stop it.

The rug is soaked.

Antonio has two diamonds in his ear; Antonio has a diamond on his sex.

Antonio shines even without the diamonds, the light from his sleep awakens me. His beauty is enormous and swallows me whole.

This is a fragment from *Jardín* that my mother highlighted for me: "I'd like to have you in such a way that, absorbed, drunk to the last drop, there wouldn't be any of you left to quench anyone else's thirst..."

April 1990

It's been several weeks since I've written. Antonio has not come back.

Osvaldo has stopped calling.

The rumors swirling about Antonio are terrible; I can't believe them. He wouldn't leave like that, without saying good-bye. I have some reels he filmed of my body, nude; in them, I'm washing, looking straight at the camera, and his voice is behind the lens. I play them on the video player and cry and cry without any solace.

What's the point of lying to my Diary?

Who am I and what do I want?

Where are you, Antonio? I'm on another Diary strike until they bring him to me, until I see his light eyes and he tells me to my face why he, too, has disappeared.

Where is he hiding and from whom? The rumors can't be true. I don't believe them.

April 21, 1990

There was a knock on the door tonight and when I opened it, I found an elderly woman, the classic grandmother from children's stories, her hair white, very beautiful. She was holding a red envelope in her hand and trembled so much as she handed it to me that she could barely control her facial muscles long enough to speak.

"Toni didn't leave, he's still in Cuba," she said.

She didn't want to come in. She kissed me and left, walking slowly through the garden.

I knew it, even as I opened it, I knew that no matter where he was when he wrote it, this would undoubtedly be his farewell.

My much missed moon,
I'm responding to your Diaries with great urgency:

I'll die one hundred times and then another hundred,
and my white bones, dust and ashes,
will keep what little is left of my soul, so very little,
a crimson nothing, in love.
—Y BANG-WON (1367–1422)

Love is a red scab when it comes to wanting you, but silence hurts less than not having you. Martí should have said: "Be free to be loved." Having my hand inside your red skirt, touching your vulva and pubic hair and your wetness and other extremes, was a separate ecstasy, or the ecstasy of being in love. I want to do it all again, even if it means having to live again. "To live life," as Portabales would say. I'm more yours every minute, without hesitation or expectations. I miss you.

Then: your navel, your tongue, your desire, your idea, your poses, to see you sitting in conversation, to take you through the house as a devotee of those spaces, to use a hat, and then your neck and your earlobes and your profile custom made to my desire, your face in flight, your fire, your umbrella, your shore, your direction, your weeping, your flower, your sperm, your prayer, your nakedness, your river, your melancholia, your fingers, the corner of your eye, your wet hair, your scheme, your support, your maneuver, your flag, your navel—again—your short nails, your nipples, your abdomen, your voice, your waking, your disgust, your fury, your choice, your majesty, you yourself, you lifting your arms off yourself, your height, your back, your fruit, your walk, your sail, your window, your rain, your sky, your century, your law, your photo, your smell of male and female as a singular species, your outline in my memory, your image when

I masturbate, your inspiration, your tastes, your anecdotes, your family and your Diary which are one and the same thing, your past, your day of birth, your pubic hair, your sound, your name peace dynamic cultural force ardor homeland infinite wait your giving birth is—will be—the common border where your smell rises in me, where I'll die one hundred and another hundred times so that I can't be anything but a guy who will look for you forever to court you, love you, kiss you, lick you, adore you, cozy you up to my belly and scream at you from the very depths of my imagination that I'm nothing without you, I want to be born again knowing you're there, poised in the memory of love. I'm still searching, searching for the way you smell, and I'm getting closer every time...

Moon, I worry, I know you'll scorn me for bothering you with these disturbing warnings—are they?—after so much damp intimacy, we shouldn't talk about what's missing from your Diary, which is the equivalent of your life. But you need to recognize facts that are worthy of attention. You can't tell the story of a life if you don't include the events that determine it. Or were you hiding to such an extreme that you never knew, for example, that certain of our officials were executed when they were found guilty of high treason, that Reagan became president after defeating Carter, that the socialist camp abandoned us, or that Alejo Carpentier died in Paris?

I don't know what I'm getting at with all this; in fact I don't know what I'm doing hooking up with "dissidents" who are considered enemies, unfortunately, first by their own definition of themselves, and then by the powers that be. I miss you, but I know I'll miss you even more later.

"The room is a space that the sculptures take on; the structures are tall: green legs rise to the ceiling, clad in mirrors shaped like rays…" Why all this? Where does it lead? Why does everyone run away when they find out about Allende's death?

Context, summary, the telling of the anecdote.

Arte Calle; what is Arte Calle? Open the door so the people might know what's going on.

Blood: Your Concept, your idea, your reflection about blood.

Ideas about blood: Since 1979, Cubans have fought in Angola in what is known as "proletarian internationalism"…we'll never know how much blood was shed. Do the raft people shed blood? How did these generals caught "drug trafficking," who were left without refuge, shed theirs? Both of Romania's dictators were executed by firing squad on Christmas Day in 1989 after a taped trial was distributed to TV stations all over the world. The deaths of Ceausescu, the Romanian president, and his wife, Elena, were part of the end of the collapse. On October 15, 1978, after a new conclave, the Polish cardinal Karol Wojtyla was elected as successor to Saint Peter, breaking the four-hundred-year tradition of only electing popes of Italian descent. On October 22, 1978, he was appointed pontiff and took on the name John Paul II. On May 13, 1981, Ali Agca shot John Paul II in St. Peter's Square. The pope almost died.

The Challenger—*the gringos' newest spaceship—exploded in '86, and the dead included a teacher; it was one of capitalism's greatest disasters. Michael Jackson had a huge hit with "Thriller." The eighties began with death and separation. John Lennon, founding member and leader of the Beatles, political and social activist, was killed outside his apartment building in New York on December 8, 1980. The entire world grieves his death; "Imagine" is played in every corner of this earthly globe and western rock and popular culture go into mourning. John Bonham, Led Zeppelin's drummer, dies from alcohol poisoning September 25, 1980, and, months later, Jimmy Page announces the group's breakup. Bob Marley, the most important figure in reggae, dies from cancer May 11, 1981. One of the greatest groups in seventies country-rock, the Eagles, announces their split in May 1982, saying they'll get back together "when hell freezes over" (meaning God only knows when they'll get back together). And where do we leave Nicaragua when the Sandinista Front loses power at the ballot box…? How many Cubans lost their lives over there? And in Panama? And what about those who died in Grenada, who we believed had been "sacrificed for the nation" but, no; now I remember the plane from*

Barbados in which the fencing team died because of sabotage, how the people, enraged and virile, cried so that injustice would tremble. Does it tremble? On December 20, the gringo army invaded Panama and whole neighborhoods disappeared. Noriega falls and there are so many deaths...Panama, Grenada, and Tortola, El Salvador, the dictatorships in Argentina, Chile, and Paraguay, the attempt on Reagan's life, the Soviet presidents. I don't know—think about all the blood and more blood that has run because of someone else's will.

Olof Palme was assassinated. As a Social Democrat, Palme had served in various posts before becoming prime minister in 1969. He had controversial points of view, criticizing the United States about the war in Vietnam, nuclear arms, and apartheid in South Africa, while defending the PLO and Fidel Castro.

His murder on February 28, 1986, remains unsolved, and there are still several theories about the crime. Christer Pettersson was charged and found guilty of the killing, but he was ultimately absolved.

A master died June 14: Jorge Luis Borges. Even though he wasn't banned outright for ideological problems in his work, his books—or copies of his books, manuscripts of his books, worn copies of his books— still circulated as if in secret, but loud enough for everyone...I remember a friend scolding me because I thought Nicolás Guillén was a better poet.

Facts to consider regarding the Berlin Wall: During its existence, a record was kept of 5,000 escapes to West Berlin; 192 people were assassinated trying to flee and another 200 were seriously injured. Among the successful flights was that of the 57 people who got out October 3, 4, and 5, 1964, through a 145-meter tunnel dug by West Berliners. The most famous failed attempt was that of Peter Fechter, who was fatally shot and bled to death before the Western media on August 17, 1962.

Products from CAME, the mutual economic aid society, included Bulgarian canned goods, stuffed pimientos from Poland, Russian meat, the little markets, and that taste, Nieve, please—that taste! Don't forget it. "Russia doesn't help us so much anymore, and we can tell." Why? 1985, Gorbachev appeared on the scene. First executive president of the USSR. Everything changed under him and here we are, still feeling the effects from afar. Sputnik, *your mother, banned words—glasnost and perestroika—disappeared from Cuba. How did we feel about that, living on Jovellar Street? Why bother with all those people born on the 11th? Wouldn't we need to know what they meant to you? "My mother now shares with me what she once didn't even dare to say." What, love? I'm saying that we need to know what your mother hid from you, and why.*

I seem to remember that we had a cosmonaut. Oh! Also, One Hundred Years of Solitude. *Don't forget the recent past, even films that made their debut just last year:*

Batman.

Cinema Paradiso.

Women on the Verge of a Nervous Breakdown.

Sex, Lies, and Videotape *(winner of the Palme d'or at Cannes)*

Dead Poets Society

Babette's Feast

Don't forget that just last October 5, the Dalai Lama was honored with the Nobel Peace Prize, and that's already history. And also: that March 7 last year, because of Salman Rushdie's Satanic Verses, *Iran broke diplomatic ties with Great Britain.*

Don't forget that things are as important as you make them. Only your body and only your soul—what's inside you—can judge me and understand what's felt on the outside, knowing that by the time you read this, I'll be in the past. Respect the past. Don't forget me.

Don't collaborate with forgetting. Hold on to the memories—even if they're vacuous—that's how it was, that's how we understood things. Where were you when everything I've just told you was happening? Where are you now that I'm away? What are you doing? Don't lie to the Diary, please, always tell the truth. It's the least you can do for yourself...Someone will tell you where I am. Where I've ended up while wanting to be there, dictating that Diary.

Whether I did right or wrong, I'll soon know. For the moment, what's important is not to forget.

I'll die one hundred times and another hundred and in all my lives I'll look like the guy who misses you—you: naked, wet, fleeing, anxious about being caught by yourself, which, in the end, preserving little or nothing of your soul, is the essence of this love match.

Your

Antonio, 1964–1990

April—I don't know which day—1990

Dear Diary:

Everyone's leaving, they all leave me behind. Some go outwards, Antonio inwards, on a stark trip between asphyxiation, claustrophobia, and a kind of must.

Images associated with a collective emotion can trap a man.

Dear Diary: Is this what we deserve? They won't trap me again; I won't stand for it.

Two diamonds—the ones that hung from Antonio's ears—come with the letter, like dragonflies; now their light is for me, and for him, a darkness that he doesn't deserve. I need somebody to tell me what to do. I'm lost, and though I may cross the street looking for him, or open the door of a movie theater to search for him, I won't see him. Everything will be in vain. He's in hiding, on an inward journey wholly unfamiliar to me. What kind of trip is this? What kind of an idea or feeling could take him like this?

I remove my old earrings, the ones Osvaldo gave me; I take them off, not without some pain. In their place, Antonio's diamonds shine like never before on this strange Havana night. The night is ours, naked "in the sky with diamonds," and I pose for him, watch his films. I eat off the plate he used, make the same recipes we ate together, I'm him and I'm me in an intimate and beautiful dance. He'll always have an unknown freedom with me.

This is the ritual of the diamonds, the ritual of light, the ritual for my memories of you.

Touché

No one could touch there
in the same way, like cracking a nut.
Like quartering life and coming back.
No one could touch there, dive so intimately,
to make a point.
We're blood kin, an extension of that
secret touch.
No one before you knew the key to my sex.
You remember my country.
I come up behind you from birth.
You have a secret touch, and when you disrobe
I feel the same holy touch of your body
ring out on my silent waist.
No one can tear us apart.

We're high,
delirious,
and Havana is out there,
waiting.

April 22, 1990

I'm on my way to my mother's house, the one on Jovellar, my house…I'm saying good-bye a little at a time. I walk on tiptoes, carefully, between puddles. Where has Osvaldo left me, now that I know Antonio exists, which means that I exist and that my body responds to me?

The street is like a scene from a film by Tomás Gutiérrez Alea. Nothing changes and everything continues. I look at the people and they look off in the distance. We're a compact mechanism, walking these salty streets. I see a newspaper and reach for it, but I never read it.

I think about Antonio, who's asked me for complete honesty in the Diary, clear waters, strength. He asks me to push myself, to be upfront about what I've shared with him. That's what I'll do. My mother has been looking for *Sputnik* magazines for a long time; she's searched all the stands in this city for that magazine she so adores, but what she finds instead are the yellow pages of a fold-out called *Cartelera*. A cultural guide to the city. A five-cent guide so we'll go to the theater and the movies and entertain our spirits with things that make time go by easier.

I try to buy an old *Sputnik* for my mother but I can't find any.

How will I find Antonio? What ritual will help me find him? Playing with fire. Playing with fear.

Who am I? What do I want? Where am I going? I'm chewing on this salty glass that's in the air in my city.

Why did Antonio appear in my life like a sign? What happens now? What are you trying to tell me?

Retelling and Confession

I spent the last few years aimed like an arrow toward him, discovering myself like a virgin every day, learning the kind of transformation that a relationship between two artists needs in order to survive. I spread like weeds when, under the sheets, he'd look for me, aroused; I'd surreptitiously frame myself in the mirror when his models opened their legs in my absence.

I learned about jealousy, and about jealousy's many disguises, about dependency and tearing apart. I began to translate lies into magnificent versions to calm my anxiety. I learned to eat using all the silverware on his glass table while sitting on the floor; I learned to use chopsticks; to seek out the most expensive perfumes.

I visited luxurious places, carpeted theaters, unknown hotels, and inaccessible offices. I never again had to leap over a wall to attend the most exclusive receptions, but I also never again felt the pleasure of swimming clandestinely in the nude at an ambassador's house.

I met mediocre people, wonderful people, mean people, powerful people, gentle and unforgettable people. I learned French and for three years I visited the "Bermuda Triangle" much too often— in other words, José Martí International Airport, where everyone disappears forever, including, not surprisingly, Osvaldo.

I left the long sessions of intimate conversation with the painter out of my Diaries. For him, I was a girl who'd arrived while still a child, a victim of my parents, a creature that needed to go through his healing process. He would restore my faith. He'd bring me into a fantasy world with his magical powers.

As part of this game, Jesús sent me a great leather coat to wear during the European winters that awaited me. From France, I received a wedding ring filled with diamonds. With it, like in fairy tales, I could travel to the ends of the earth.

I seldom went back to my old neighborhood. It was part of the ritual, an eternal part of the past. It was a terrible rejection of what I'd been, a threat in the air of what I could become again. Fear that the chariot would turn into a pumpkin and that I'd sink my black corduroy shoes in the mud on those crumbling and dirty streets.

I always liked to talk with my mother, to listen together to her staticky programs, with the old sones and aged, decadent boleros. Whenever I left her, I had to learn all over again how to be Osvaldo's Nieve, but Osvaldo was too far away and I often recited Rimbaud's verses to orient myself, because there was no new news from that other France. I was alone for so long, ensconced in somebody else's mansion, isolated from the truth, from what happens on this island, interned away from reality. I got many telephone calls from friends, from those who'd stayed. Out there, they went to bed without eating, and I remained still, incapable of doing anything. Thinking only of setting sail and leaving, leaving everything behind, without considering the consequences.

I, Nieve Guerra, was a replicant. I cried and redid my makeup, cried and redid my makeup. I wandered and presaged that letters were dangerous and that my wings were too big for the mansion in which Osvaldo had deposited me. I came and went from art shows and wrote astronomical checks while I silently stole food from the mansion's pantry to take to my mother, without Osvaldo's permission. The money wasn't mine. His patrimony wasn't mine. His world was not my world. The maps and letters from Paris spoke of another life: Café Capuchino and Place d'Italie, the Bastille and La Villette. In fact, Osvaldo shivered in Paris while I died of heat saying good-bye to the last of my friends who'd stayed and were now leaving Havana.

I said good-bye on countless mornings. On the way home, as we rounded the cemetery, I saw Arte Calle's graffiti slowly get covered up on the walls where I'd cut myself painting, those walls censored in a hasty and fearful act.

I fell in love with Antonio and I substituted him for my hero in the distance, epic and cruel; I was cyclical and desperate. In his silence, Osvaldo fell apart. Antonio grew before my eyes, grew in courage when he gave up his freedom and my love for something so tangible and real. They both left me.

One left for Paris and the other disappeared inward. Sometimes it's preferable to believe in confinement instead of the world. But it depends on what each fate might mean to each person.

With Antonio I learned that a woman and a country need to be inhabited, touched, lived in, even if the price is a constant and somber abandonment.

It's December 24 again. But Christmas doesn't exist, not like twenty years ago in Güines, where I was born. Twenty eternal years have passed in my mother's life and it seems that she finally understands that she shouldn't wait for Christmas. We have to get used to the neighborhood, to the crumbling street and the mud in front of Jovellar #111. Your talent doesn't matter, nor your erudition; you have to master poverty because you're paying for your absolute loyalty and nobility. That all has a price.

The house was dark, my mother had slept until noon. I woke her up, but I could see in her eyes that she was hiding something. A

terrible silence ran through the house. There were no visitors and—
the weirdest thing of all—I couldn't find the radio anywhere. But
my eyes registered the anomaly in an instant: it's a very small space,
there are not a lot of places to hide a piece of Russian junk that size.

"It's broken."

I didn't understand a thing.

"Broken, broken."

I didn't believe a word she said. My mother was lying for a
reason. I opened the cabinets, I shuffled through my things, in
the drawers and boxes and, finally, I found the radio wrapped in a
sheet. I plugged it in and it worked fine, like always.

My mother made coffee and tuned in to Radio Martí, the
enemy station. It broadcasts from Miami and it's as clear as it's ever
been in spite of the interferences. My mother, pale, drank her coffee
like an automaton. We spent an hour in silence.

"Yes, well, no, thank you, dear, leave that be, that's okay, I'll do
that, there's no water."

Finally, the news came on. An announcer talked about
Osvaldo and then Osvaldo talked about himself. As he always
does, he told truths and lies. He described himself like a hero. He
really knows how to manipulate reality in his favor. He manages it
in the same way he works and diffuses his figures: "a little texture
here, a little texture there." His hands behind his back, and dark

glasses over his eyes to make it harder to distinguish the lie on his face.

The announcer talked about his French girlfriend, about the shelter she'd provide for him from now on. Osvaldo was staying in Paris forever, he was leaving me behind, he was closing the door in my face. I don't exist on the news when they talk about him.

He said good-bye while the news continued with today's more important headlines. I'd said good-bye to him the day I undressed for Antonio; I'd said good-bye months before, when I stopped believing that Paris wasn't so far from Havana.

My mother talked about political asylum, statements, treason, cowardice. I talked about vertigo, an abyss, loneliness, madness. The telephone wouldn't stop ringing. A few friends had begun to arrive.

I couldn't believe what was happening. I'd be interrogated, singled out, crucified. There's nothing worse than being abandoned. Politics was once more getting mixed up with love. It was my father's story, and Fausto's, and Antonio's. It came back like an unavoidable cycle, always haunting the female lineage in this Caribbean socialism that no one can figure out.

Everyone hugged me. The pity, fear, and compassion disgusted me. Our friends talked in low voices: anyone could be listening to our conversation. Again with the paranoia, which signals I'm in familiar territory.

Ten o'clock at night. Two strangers in civilian clothes showed up; they look like the type of guys who don't have many friends. They came to ask questions, to verify, to play with other people's pain. Our friends left me alone because no one could save me from the interrogation. I can just imagine what I looked like, because I saw it reflected in my mother's terrified face. There were intruders in our home; luckily, we had been waiting for them. At least I didn't have to go anywhere.

It's obvious that I'm the only one who's affected by this: the nation, Cuban painting, officialdom—nobody's hurt like me. I didn't say anything about Osvaldo. My training also includes shame and loyalty. Besides, I was the last to know, they can't do anything to me. Now I won't have further contact with this "citizen."

They asked for my passport. I had it in my bag, and it would have been childish at this point to pretend to hide it. I tried to avoid a search. When I handed over my papers, I was also giving up my pass to the rest of the world. Everything I'd lived through with Osvaldo to that point had been a movie and it was fading with that gray document, which could no longer contain my hopes. I saw it vanish with my own eyes, unable to refuse to give it up, and with it any chance of escape. Good-bye Paris, good-bye world.

The house search lasted four hours. They didn't find anything except radio programs and unfinished poems. They left the apartment a disaster, but they never found the banned books.

I never went back to Nuevo Vedado. They sealed the house immediately, so it was impossible for me to go and pick up my things. It's possible that those things never really belonged to me anyway; in a way, I'd known that since the moment Antonio first touched them. It's a good thing this Diary is so small. That's why it survives; I can carry it anywhere. I didn't cry. I didn't cry because I've already cried too much over the same losses. In a way, I should be used to all this; it's been this way since I was born. It's perfectly logical that everything should turn out this way. What else could I have expected? I've lived my life with truncated travel, men who leave without saying good-bye, plans that die waiting for permits, and laws made in a panic.

I looked at my mother. She was going on like it was ten years ago, crying in a corner, disillusioned, tired, and skinnier than ever. I stared right at her because I didn't want to ever forget that moment. Now it was my turn to be disenchanted; she'd known about this before it even happened.

I remembered the time when Osvaldo and I went all over the city, flying between cars, ignoring every single ideology and the name of every country and all systems of governance. We were tied together, dependent on a passion that couldn't be vain, couldn't be mortal, couldn't ever produce headlines for a foreign radio station. I kicked the radio and ran out the door, down Jovellar, down Aramburu, Soledad, and Marina Streets, until I got to Maceo Park. I crossed the avenue, zigzagging through traffic, and scaled the seawall at the Malecón the same way I'd climbed the wall at the ambassador's house, the way I'd done when I was sixteen and looking for Osvaldo without even knowing him yet. Now it was too late. I know this feeling too well, and it will haunt me forever.

I touched the wall. I looked at the icy December waters. I saw my face in the clear pool and found myself nude once more in this familiar ritual. First my shoes, my underwear last. I couldn't calculate the distance that separated me from him. I didn't look back. I didn't breathe deep or consider the consequences. I dove into the sea, my body charging against the cutting and frigid depths that once more welcomed me.

Order, peace, and silence, that's what I felt while I was immersed. Then I went up, up, for no reason. I got closer to the light and returned to the surface; this is where I'm from. I emerged slowly, surveying my surroundings, but making sure water covered my face, separating, detaching my fate from reality. Suddenly, a white rain began to fall on the sea. It was snow. It snowed very lightly, only for me, and only for a few seconds. The water froze little by little.

I opened my arms and legs to swim, to escape, to reach Osvaldo, or Fausto, or my father. I wanted to flee to the open sea but I was trapped, numb with cold. I held on to Antonio's voice, which supported me.

I'm still alive, snow on snow. I'm now a rock made of ice with a bit of algae, a few mollusks, wrinkled papers, and some sand. I wander aimlessly toward total stagnation.

I'm in Havana, and I try, I try to go forward, a little each day. But once the Caribbean freezes, there's no chance of going anywhere. Over here, I continue to write in my Diary, wintering with my thoughts, unable to move, condemned forever to be in the very same place.

About the Author

A child star launched by a role as host of a popular children's radio and television news program in Cuba, Wendy Guerra was inspired by her own diaries, written as a child during Cuba's revolution. Published in eight languages, *Everyone Leaves* won the first Brugera Prize as well as the Premio Cabaret Del Caribe in 2009. Guerra lives and writes in Cuba, her home and primary source of inspiration.

About the Translator

Photo courtesy DePauw University

Achy Obejas is the author of various books, including the award-winning novel *Days of Awe* and the best-selling poetry chapbook *This Is What Happened in Our Other Life*. She edited the critically acclaimed *Havana Noir* crime-fiction anthology and translated (into Spanish) Junot Diaz's *The Brief Wondrous Life of Oscar Wao*. She is a founding member of the Creative Writing Faculty at the University of Chicago, a member of the Editorial Board of In These Times, the editorial advisory board of the Great Books Foundation, and a blogger for WBEZ.org. She was born in Havana and continues to spend extended time there.

Made in the USA
Charleston, SC
11 November 2012